"These delightfully original stories wear their insights and humor with ease, as if it were no great feat to be so casually, splendidly wise. Jane Gillette is an intrepid and often wickedly funny writer. She cracks open each story to guide us to new, sometimes hard, always surprising places, like one of her own characters "taking [her] psychic pulse and finding in it the heartbeat of the world.""

—DAPHNE KALOTAY, author of *Sight Reading*

"Jane Gillette's *The Trail of the Demon* is one of the best discoveries I've made in years. Wise, observant, and refreshingly unmannered, Gillette's retrospective stories insist that the past is always alive in the present and that none of our experience is negligible. Be prepared to fall under her spell. A wonderful collection."

—ANTHONY VARALLO, author of *Everyone Was There*

"Jane Gillette's stories are wry forays into venerated institutions such as academia, publishing, locavorism, and middle age. Her characters are eccentric truth-tellers, great wits and observers, dinner party companions you'd fight to sit next to even as you were a bit afraid of them."

—TINA MAY HALL, author of *The Physics of Imaginary Objects*

"The nimble, learned narrators in Jane Gillette's first collection of stories often call upon literary classics as they detail classic reckonings from childhood to older age. *The Trail of the Demon* thrills the reader with its replete control of language and culture and history. Like Henry James, Gillette worries constricted moments until they release their larger truths, but the whimsical touch and gimlet eye are uniquely her own."

—NANCY ZAFRIS, author of *The Home Jar*

"I love these stories by Jane Gillette. I felt taken in hand by a smart, sophisticated storyteller, her voice assured—both simple and elegant. I love the playful ways she takes in the reader, relating the real to the mythic and fictional. I like the way she builds one dramatic arc and then allows a new element to enter—challenging her to integrate both into a single story. I enjoy the way she implies elements of social conflict—class, race, work—without strain. I like her comfort with sexuality, so often part of the story. Some of the stories are, like 'The Trail of the Demon,' superb. All are delightful."

—JOHN J. CLAYTON, author of *Many Seconds into the Future*

THE TRAIL OF THE DEMON AND OTHER STORIES

BY JANE GILLETTE

The Trail of the Demon and Other Stories

By Jane Gillette

Edited by Speer Morgan

Associate Editors

Bailey Boyd	Brooks Holton
Brooke Butler	Jennifer McCauley
Gwendolyn Edward	Rose Nash
Katelyn Freund	Maurine Pfuhl
Carley Gomez	

Missouri Review Books

Published by Missouri Review Books
357 McReynolds Hall, University of Missouri
Columbia, Missouri, 65211

Missouri Review Books is published by the *Missouri Review* through the College of
Arts & Science of the University of Missouri, with private contributions.

ISBN: 978-1-945829-06-2 (print)
ISBN: 978-1-945829-07-1 (digital)

Library of Congress Control Number: 2017940283

www.missourireview.com

Cover Image: "Faust's Vision," Luis Ricardo Falero, 1878 © Private Collection/
Bridgeman Images

For Mr. Rose

Table of Contents

Foreword.. ix

A Preface for Mrs. Parry 1
First published in the Yale Review, Fall 1987

Divine Afflatus 11
*First published in the Michigan Quarterly Review,
Summer 2008*

Judas and the Slave Girl..................................... 23
First published in the Hopkins Review, Summer 2011

Sins against Animals.. 47
First published in the Virginia Quarterly Review, Fall 1988

The Ring and the Box It Came In 63
*First published in the Michigan Quarterly Review,
Spring 2009*

Meditation XXXI: On Sustenance 77
First published in the Missouri Review, Winter 2013

Atlas Shrugging 93
First published in Zyzzyva, Summer 2012

The Ghost Driver 105
First published in the Antigonish Review, Spring 2014

The Odor of Mr. Fitzpatrick............................... 115
First published in the Antigonish Review, Winter 2012

Visiting.. 123
First published in the Missouri Review, Fall 2013

Irene 131
First published in the Hopkins Review, Summer 2015

The Trail of the Demon 145
First published in the Missouri Review, Fall 2014

Foreword

One of the hallmarks of fine writing is that it often reminds you of other great writing while having its own voice. Jane Gillette's short stories remind me of Alice Munro's in showing both seriousness and levity and in moving freely in time from the past to the future, eventually finding the long view. Like Munro's stories, Gillette's are concerned with the inexorable march of time in her characters' lives and with those odd and remarkable moments when everything comes together in a way that is not limited to the mundane world—epiphanies that point beyond in surprising fashion.

Gillette is also reminiscent of another great realist, F. Scott Fitzgerald. Despite being most famous for his novels—one of which was recognized after his death as among America's greatest—Fitzgerald actually made his living as a successful writer of short fiction and a not-so-successful screenwriter. Gillette's stories, like Fitzgerald's, are concerned with the slipperiness of class identity. In both *The Great Gatsby* and his stories, Fitzgerald was fascinated by the impenetrability of the class system—"rich girls don't marry poor boys"—while Gillette is more intrigued by the simultaneous importance and meaninglessness of that system. Many of her characters are concerned with symbols of wealth and class—with the Seven Sisters or Yale or rich or not-so-rich marriages, with inheritances or the lack thereof—yet finally these characters come to see the dubious significance of such trappings.

In ways that are partly circumstantial, Gillette also reminds me of Edith Wharton. Wharton is thought of as a late starter because she didn't publish her first novel until she was forty, although much earlier she had published her first short stories and written a best-selling classic on interior design and architecture. Gillette, too, was less known as a writer of fiction than of historic preservation, design, and finally landscape design, although she started publishing short stories about the same time in her life as did Wharton. Wharton's novel *The House of Mirth* has been called a naturalistic novel in its concern with the destructiveness of the American class system, particularly for women, as its heroine, Lily Bart, slides from being the ingénue of the season to poverty and death. Gillette is equally interested in such plain concerns as class and social identity, but in ways that are nearly postmodern in their awareness of paradox and absurdity.

In the title story of this collection, "The Trail of the Demon," a Washington, D.C., woman succumbs to both revenge and racist thoughts after being mugged one evening. Dawn is a middle-aged woman who takes up running for fitness and one day is grabbed and sexually threatened by a black teenager. Dawn's response is not fear but anger, partly because as a teacher she has led a long life of political correctness and community involvement. She runs after her attacker with a broken glass bottle but is unable to catch him. Afterward, she is stunned by her own response, which over time is memorialized in a local folktale emblematic of racism. "A Preface for Mrs. Parry" is another story that suggests that actual events, memory, and myth often ride along together, making none of them either quite real or true. Not only do relationships and even marriages become insignificant over time, but some of our most important personal memories may be so affected by self-mythologizing as to represent desire more than fact.

In "Irene," the protagonist has a pet bird, Buck, named after a lost love, which escapes from her house and flies to a tree. Irene tries to talk Buck into staying with her, and the cockatiel serves as a friend, lover, and priest in whom Irene confides, seeking penance for a past she never resolved. As Irene recounts her life to Buck, the voices of the bird and of the man she once loved blur and intertwine. The story is masterfully told, a stirring meditation on fantasy, forgiveness, and grace.

In "Visiting," Judith and Alicia are old friends. Alicia, wife of an Episcopal priest, is dying of cancer, and Judith goes guiltily to visit her in the hospice. Judith remembers hearing that "Jesus commands us to visit the sick and pray for them when they die," and though she's shaky regarding her feelings about religion, she feels a moral imperative. To entertain Alicia, she fabricates an anecdotal tale about an impromptu affair with a man whom she vividly and believably describes as the best lover she has ever had. Alicia is captivated, while Judith feels a bit guilty for creating such a fiction, yet the story's conclusion takes it all a step beyond in suggesting the need to create the perfect story, both in life and religion.

"Meditation XXXI: On Sustenance" tells about a West Coast landscape architect and his natural-foods-advocate wife who relocate to Indiana to start a restaurant specializing in locally grown food. The successful husband fully embraces his wife's vision of starting a locavore restaurant, and the two put their all into it, only to have that vision come crashing down around them. It is a tale with the feel of parable about how a noble ambition tinged with arrogance or blindness can end in disappointment.

"Divine Afflatus" is the story of a poet whose whole career is based on his dead son, killed in a car accident at age eight. His son's death is central to the poet's later work, which is praised by others but contributes to the poet's own self-hatred. It eventually leads to his divorce and subsequent move into a row house next to a woman who dislikes him due to his habit of chain-smoking and their shared thin walls. Unaware of his past or his status as a Yale Younger poet, she publicly shames him. Told through two perspectives, "Divine Afflatus" is at once about how personal tragedies become the lens through which we see the world and about how the world may refuse to soften, even for the suffering.

In "Judas and the Slave Girl," a thirteen-year-old girl in Muncie, Indiana, falls in love with her dance teacher. A kid who knows almost more than she should, she is both foolish and knowledgeable, and within the retrospective frame of the story she learns the insignificance of such early personal melodramas. These and the other stories in the collection are all concerned with friendships or primary relationships, with the importance and fallibility of a person's memory and sense of self, and, finally, with the fact that the long view often contradicts what seems the most important concern at any moment.

I admire the fact that all of Gillette's stories are compellingly honest about the nature of memory and personal history. I admire their fullness and humaneness. Her book kicks off the Missouri Review Books series of must-publish books. We are especially proud that this is Jane's debut collection, a fact that illustrates our commitment to helping launch new writers of all ages and ethnicities.

Speer Morgan

A Preface for Mrs. Parry

In the fall of 1965, my first year as a graduate student at Yale, I was forced to take an undergraduate Latin review class that met at eight in the morning. If I made a ninety or above, this grade would replace my failing score on the Latin reading comprehension test and thus fulfill part of the English Department's language requirement. My adviser could not imagine how I had managed to forget four years of high school Latin in just four years of college. "It doesn't seem possible," he frowned—but it was, for they were gone.

The very symmetry of time explained their disappearance to my not-so-logical mind. And of course I knew—as my adviser did not—what insubstantial years they had been: Caesar, obscured by hormonal fluctuations; Virgil, construed to the tunes of *American Bandstand*; Cicero, interrupted by Junior Classical League activities designed to bring a dead language alive to the teenaged mind. No wonder I took advantage of college to expunge Latin from my memory altogether.

I did not want to take this Latin review class, but—*mirabile dictu*—it turned out to be my favorite course. Not that it was intellectually stimulating; in fact, it was unusually dull. Nor was it particularly useful, for as soon as I looked at the grade, my regained knowledge evaporated from my mind completely. That was on a cold day in February, and I could almost hear it sizzle out the top of my head, like steam. Hence, it's difficult to say why I liked the class so much, except for my teacher.

She calmly, carefully led us through Latin review, first through the grammar, then through a little Ovid. She also taught us, retaught us, to scan. I don't suppose we learned a lot of Latin, yet I found the class a comfortable reaching out toward something, comfortable just because

1

the reaching was destined to fall short. A great barrier seemed to stand between our feeble efforts and the perfection of a dead language. It was like putting a hand to the belly of a pregnant woman to feel at a brief distance the warm, solid kick of life shut safely away from the touch of the world.

As for my teacher, I cannot remember whether she was tall or short, fat or thin, pretty or plain, young or old. To the eye of a twenty-two-year-old, everything between thirty and fifty looks the same; my impression, however, is that she was about thirty-five. I retain a vague impression of her manner—one of calm, cool thoroughness. I infer that she must have been kind, simply because she was the only professor I had at Yale who didn't scare me to death. As a result of not being frightened, I found myself able to listen to her criticism, to almost hear what she was saying.

This became particularly important in October when I failed the first hour test. I got a fifty, and she pointed out that the half of the test I had managed to complete was perfect down to the last long mark.

I, in turn, told her about *Sputnik*, which the Russians had put into space during my first year of Latin at McKinley Junior High School. After our shame was announced to the world, I lay awake far into the night, vowing that I would always put the long marks in the right place—a sign to me at the time of absolute intellectual integrity.

I think that she laughed at my anecdote and then suggested that I relax a little. I should keep in mind, she said, that if I had enough time, I could do everything perfectly, but if I didn't have enough time, then I might have to compromise.

This advice sounded sensible to me. The final exam would be three hours long. That should give me more than enough time.

One might wonder, of course, whether I had missed the point of her remarks, which I've put into indirect discourse because I have no memory of her actual words. Might I not have created the wider connotations of her remarks after the fact? Perhaps, although I think that this is what she did imply—the imperfecting pressures of limited time. I am sure that, even though at the moment I was desperately trying to avoid these implications—even to the point of misunderstanding her words—I was nevertheless dutifully recording them in my memory for future indirect reference.

At that time in my life, I was struggling for perfection as strenuously as if the struggle itself would make up for a life that had been spent largely in ignoring where the long marks went. I am no doubt exaggerating a bit, even now, because I had not in truth had time to accumulate a desperate amount of intellectual sin. Still, I had undoubtedly been guilty of slackness. I am an only child, and I suppose my parents had conveyed to me their expectations that I be perfect at the same time that, neither intellectual nor industrious themselves, they had conveyed no notions of how to achieve perfection. They actually seemed to believe that I could excel at everything without effort. I at once believed this and yet, during college, grew increasingly afraid to do anything wholeheartedly lest I incur the failure I knew I deserved.

I had applied to graduate school because I couldn't think of anything else to do, and I arrived in New Haven that fall feeling conspicuously stupid. The C I'd gotten in political science, my failure to make Phi Beta Kappa, and my inability to achieve a degree higher than *magna* provided premonitions of a disaster toward which I felt myself aimlessly drifting. Furthermore, I had never managed to fall in love with anyone who fell in love with me. My gestures of romance had been, by and large, reserved for a preppy blond lacrosse player— destined to become a successful investment banker—who had married the first of his series of industrial heiresses the previous summer. Meanwhile, my mother—an elementary school teacher wed to an auditor for a shoe company—wondered out loud and in public why, if I was so smart, I hadn't managed to marry someone rich.

It was then and there that I decided to turn over a new leaf.

I took Anglo-Saxon, American Literature, and Modernism—in addition to the Latin review class—and for once in my life, I read every single word of assignments and all of the footnotes in articles and books; I read the numbers at the bottom of each page, and I even took notes in class. I also counted every calorie I ate and listed them in a notebook, limiting myself to eight hundred a day. These magical precautions enclosed me in a nimbus of good luck, I believed, so that soon, although rather far behind, I was doing well, undeniably well, except for that fifty on the hour test, which I knew I could more than make up for on the final—given three hours in which to achieve perfection. By the end of November, I had come to feel that in many ways my mediocre self had already ceased to exist.

Then a strange thing happened to me one morning before Latin class. We met in a room near the offices of the Classics Department— located in Winchester Hall, a dark Victorian pile that overlooked the

Grove Street Cemetery, where for centuries New Haven had buried her most respectable citizens. I never ate breakfast before class, only treated myself to a cup of double-strength instant coffee (zero calories!) so that by the time I climbed up to the Classics Department, I felt perfect—so lightheaded and peaceful, so pure and nonexistent that I could hear my heart beating outside my body, throbbing along the dirty dark-green walls, knocking at the office doors. I leaned my forehead against the hall window to recover my breath. I snuffed in the comforting smell of chalk and floor polish and thoughts as dry as dust. Against my skin, the window felt surprisingly warm for a mid-December morning.

Over the scaly head of a gargoyle, I looked down into a graveyard surrounded by a high stone wall. Off to the left was the gate to the cemetery, a monumental arch of red sandstone squarely modeled after the Egyptian. It seemed as if it should say ABANDON ALL HOPE, but I knew it said, THE DEAD SHALL BE RAISED. There was actually a period carved into the arch. THE DEAD SHALL BE RAISED PERIOD. This religious pronouncement mingled conviction with complacency and thereby set a certain tone for the secular university that radiated out from it. So many statements at Yale, it seemed to me, were followed by PERIOD. That the statement also suggested a certain passive acceptance on the part of the dead was so much a part of the ethos, I don't think I even took notice of it at the time.

The air was as hazy as October, filled with the warm yellow light that falls through autumn's elms—even though the trees were bare now and the cemetery coated with their brown relics, through which the gravestones stuck up like widely spaced, slightly discolored teeth: monuments not to heroes but to the everyday dead of New Haven who had chewed their way through blameless lives. And yet, even they were not infinitely patient, infinitely faithful, for above the stones, heaving and flowing in visible layers, the air hung in motes so thick that it looked as if the dusty dead had given up on Jesus and were rising of their own accord, particle by particle, upward to a heaven that welcomed them by its very parallel of layered soft gray clouds. For a second, against all reason, I saw an act of free will on the part of the forgotten dead.

Beautifully the souls rose up in gently shifting currents of smoke, for in the next second, I saw the fire and then the gardener, an old man, the eternal janitor who sweeps up after the inevitable. He leaned on his rake in a narrow patch of bared grass and watched his smoldering pile. Heaped up with wet trophies, the fire languished, too feeble to flare and consume, and the smoke struggled out into undulating layers that hung around as if awaiting some definitive event.

That was a great moment in my life, whatever it meant to me then, however leaden it seems to me now. The moment before, I was the way I was; the moment after, for no good reason, I was all there, hungry, and no longer hell-bent on perfection. Of course, I wish I could say that afterward I became a brilliant scholar as well as a sensible adult and that my subsequent years at Yale were happy and successful, but in truth, I only became what I had been before, a haphazard student— who has nevertheless managed to live entangled in the net of my frailty for an additional fifty years. Given where I was headed, I consider this no mean feat, and so, from time to time, I still think of this moment, although with no additional insight. Compared to it, opening my first-semester grades was nothing. I discovered that I'd gotten three Honors—and I could now say that it was by work and not by magic. My Latin teacher had given me a ninety, and that was a gift, one way or another, for even if I had earned every point of it, I am sure she added affection to what students deserved. And if I hadn't earned every point of it, I'm sure she gave me the benefit of the doubt with a generosity that overrode her scholarly love of exactitude.

A year or so later, I watched the wreckers tear down Winchester Hall. A big iron ball slammed into a wall, which presumably crumbled, for the dust rose immediately, far thicker and uglier and yet not totally unlike the smoke of that December morning's leaves. It was as if the ball had punctured a container of dust and ashes and set them free for all the world to see. Or at least that's how I saw it, for despite the Latin review class, my vision of the classics was controlled by the usual clichés. As I recall, a professor I knew stood near me. An Old Blue, a New Critic, a strong Catholic, he watched the wreckage with different, perhaps fresher, eyes than mine. He had saved a gargoyle from destruction, and it leered at me from the protection of his embrace. I found myself wishing him bad dreams for having intervened to save it; better dust and ashes, I thought, than salvation to no appointed end. I also remember catching a glimpse of my Latin teacher in the crowd.

Some years later, in 1970 or so, at my then husband's fifth Yale reunion, I slipped away from a party with the man who was the love of my life, the only man I've ever loved. He was beautiful and charming as well as vain, and he didn't love me back, but even so, he was quite an adventuresome soul. I think the party was at the Yale Commons—I can't quite remember—but I know we hadn't far to go. We dodged quickly around the block and in through the gate of the Grove Street Cemetery, where we consummated my love on the grave of Mathala Russell.

*

The odd thing about all of this is that for over a decade, I distinctly remembered my teacher as having been named Mrs. Parry—Anne Amory Parry, Mrs. Adam Milman Parry. Given this clue, Homerists will begin to suspect why I have chosen a preface in which to remember her so imperfectly. Mrs. Parry had married into a family of classicists whose work—like her own—focused on the Homeric question, one of those scholarly issues that have been debated for several centuries yet admit of no answer. The question pertains to the origin of the *Iliad* and the *Odyssey*; for more than a hundred years it centered around the conflict between the Analysts (the poems are conglomerated layers surviving from different eras) and the Unitarians (the poems were written by Homer). In the late 1920s, the debate was revolutionized by Milman Parry, who suggested that the Homeric poet (or poets) composed the poem orally from a traditional hoard of formulae. From his work has sprung another century of fruitful disagreements among a wide range of scholars. How Milman Parry would himself have developed his theory will never be known because in 1935, at the age of thirty-three, he shot himself—by accident, some say, because few want to imagine a scholar committing suicide on the verge of his fame.

My statement here is rough, possibly even slightly inaccurate, but for the curious, the matter is beautifully set forth in Adam Parry's preface to his father's collected essays, *The Making of Homeric Verse* (Oxford, 1971). Shortly after writing this preface, Adam Parry was killed in a motorcycle accident in France. The motorcycle was going a hundred miles an hour, and everyone has found it difficult to imagine why a promising scholar would have driven so recklessly down a road in France on the verge of a great career. Whatever the answer to the questions surrounding the deaths of Milman and Adam Parry, my imagination remains focused on Mrs. Parry, who—beyond intention and control—was riding behind her husband on the same motorcycle.

One of the few things I actually know about Mrs. Parry is that she wrote a monograph called *Blameless Aegisthus* after a famous crux in the first book of the *Odyssey*. The Homeric narrator calls Aegisthus "blameless" in his introduction to a speech by Zeus. In the speech, however, Zeus puts responsibility for murder and adultery on Aegisthus's shoulders. The gods had specifically warned Aegisthus, through their messenger, Hermes Argeiphontes, not to kill Agamemnon and not to take Clytemnestra for his wife; if he did, Orestes would come to claim his patrimony and exact his revenge. Clearly, in Zeus's eye, Aegisthus is anything but blameless, and at no point does the Homeric narrator explicitly contradict Zeus. For example, he does not excuse Aegisthus, too young to have been fed to his father, Thyestes, by his uncle Atreus, on the grounds that he was effecting his own revenge on his cousin Agamemnon, Atreus's son. The narrator, like Zeus, finds Aegisthus full of blame regardless of his family history.

The Parryists would argue that the Homeric poet, hastily grasping for an adjective, found a rhythmic suitability in *amymonos Aigisthoio*, and to hell with the meaning. Mrs. Parry, however, disagreed with this interpretation and spent her scholarly effort trying to prove not that Aegisthus was morally flawless, that is, without blame, but that *amymon* meant something else, something like *fair* or *handsome*—that is, physically flawless. One can see such a redefinition as a bold whack at the Gordian knot or as an attempt to duck the issue. In either case, I suppose Mrs. Parry settled for an imperfect solution.

Like most people, I find that Aeschylus, rather than Homer, has impressed his image of Aegisthus on my memory: a vain sort, full of himself, drawn into the web of Clytemnestra's passions as surely as was Agamemnon, weak as well as full of blame. And beautiful? I don't know. But no doubt Clytemnestra thought so. She loved him. And he, her. Perhaps only we are left—the nonheroic, the antitragic, the imperfectly beautiful—to look anachronistically for the force that drives a human being into the circumference of a desperate mate, the tangled net that ties many a lover onto the back of many a motorcycle. Not even a bloody family history, just a blameless force.

Do I really think that Mrs. Parry died for love?

I don't know. I really know nothing about Mrs. Parry. In fact, I have never laid eyes on Mrs. Parry, for my distinct memory of having her for a teacher was a mistake. And yet, even though I now know that she was not my teacher and even suspect how my memory went astray, the implications of Mrs. Parry refuse to disappear. Mine is a memory of Yale as the *Iliad* is a memory of Troy.

*

Not long ago, a close friend of mine came across an obituary of the Parrys in an old classical journal and rushed to tell me that when Anne Amory married Adam Parry in April 1966, she resigned from the Yale Classics Department and so could hardly have taught me Latin in 1965 under the name of Mrs. Parry. A few days later, I had someone check my Yale transcript: I had taken Latin from Kaufman, whoever she was, Mrs. or Miss. Her name brought not a single image to my mind. And yet this was unmistakable proof. Why, then, did my memory place Mrs. Parry so firmly in that classroom?

I have thought about this a great deal, for it is really much more pleasant to think about than many other things, and as best I can recall, Mrs. Parry assumed her place in my memory one day in the 1970s when I was having lunch in the Jesuit Dining Room with the head of the Georgetown Classics Department. Surrounded by tables of black-garbed priests, I told him about the wonderful Latin class I'd taken my first year of graduate school at Yale. My description was undoubtedly more circumspect than the one I have inscribed above because so many of the details were inappropriate to the presentation of a lunchtime self. I could not call my teacher by name.

I think that my listener, conceivably bored but ever polite, said, in a reply vaguely aimed at Yale and classics, that it was a shame about the Parrys.

It was during the explanation of this non sequitur that Mrs. Parry made her leap into my memory. My actual teacher—whose name had already vanished—was replaced completely by a woman I had never seen or even heard of before that moment. I say that she leaped. In truth, she strolled across on a bridge of rotten logic: It seemed perfectly reasonable to me that any woman teacher whom I had liked so much at Yale would have been killed in a terrible accident in France. In subsequent years, further details only confirmed this notion, and even today, even as I write this, in my memory Mrs. Parry continues to crawl onto the back of the motorcycle and roar off to meet her fate, and I continue to follow her in pity and awe but with no chance of understanding that final event.

We all live on the breath of an accident and sing about our memories in a language ever struggling to be born, and because I was self-absorbed and young to the point of cliché, I will never remember anything real about my actual Latin teacher. Worse, aware and more than middle-aged, I do not regret that I fail to remember her, wonderful though she was. She rests in peace. Instead, I regret that I do not remember Mrs. Parry. Perhaps it is only the nature of tragic heroes and heroines to capture our memories and keep our darkest fears fresh and green, and yet I wish I had actually seen Mrs. Parry, I wish I had actually known her, I wish I remembered something real about her, for as it is I am destined to be pursued forever by an image of Mrs. Parry: seated on the back of the motorcycle, hurtling into the future, along for the ride and holding on for dear life, like a footnote to someone else's text.

Divine Afflatus

When Johnson's son was eight, he ran out into the street after a ball and died instantly: hit by a car. A terrible tragedy for the family. Johnson had two daughters and a wife he felt estranged from even before the accident. A few years later, Johnson's unassuageable grief finally precipitated the divorce. His wife found his physical presence unbearable now that his mind was always absent, brooding on the boy. His daughters felt themselves less essential than ever. Johnson eventually remarried, and this constellation of events—divorce, remarriage, his daughters' stunted lives, all revolving around that one unobserved but ever-to-be-imagined moment of the rolling ball, the blond child, and the car—controlled his life in a way that would have been impossible had he been a lawyer, say, or a stockbroker. Because he was a poet, the accident became the focus of his work. Someone once counted at a reading, and fully half of Johnson's poems made reference in one way or another to the accident. It was not so much the boy himself as his death, plus his daughters' reactions, Johnson's own grief and suffering, the divorce, and the healing remarriage, that formed the core of Johnson's work.

Johnson flourished professionally, and although some complained that his poems were too limpid, no one disputed that they were unusually musical and moving, particularly when Johnson recited them at poetry readings, as he frequently did. In fact, he was better known for his reading than for his writing, although, like many a contemporary poet, he was not much known for either.

Johnson made his actual living by teaching English at the university, and one afternoon, he held an extra class to go over some poems the students had not had time to discuss the previous day. Although the class was optional, lots of students showed up, and since it went well, Johnson was feeling rather pleased with himself: popular and successful as a teacher—a pleasant bonus to being a good if little-known poet. He was in a cheerful mood as he drove home along a winding commuter route, but the day took a sharp turn for the worse when he saw a blond child wandering along the grassy strip that separated the sidewalk from the busy street. The boy was under three, far too young to be outside alone, and totally oblivious to danger.

Johnson pulled over immediately and parked his car at a safe distance from the boy. He wanted to be calm and slow and smooth in all his motions so that he didn't frighten the child into flight. A little beyond the boy sat a golden retriever, who at the sight of Johnson got up and moved farther down the block at a leisurely pace, heading toward the corner, trailing his feathery tail behind him like a lure. The child followed the dog calmly, slowly, close to—perhaps only a foot away from—the road. No other cars stopped; none even slowed down. Johnson felt doomed to creep eternally after the blond child, who followed the reddish-gold flume of the dog's tail, death whizzing by indifferent at his side.

As the dog turned the corner, Johnson called out softly to the boy, who stopped immediately and turned around. Although the name Johnson called was not his, the child seemed pleased to see Johnson—the dog was gone now—and with what seemed like a gleam of recognition started slowly forward to meet him. Johnson slowly edged over onto the sidewalk and gently extended a welcoming hand. The boy likewise changed his trajectory, edging farther from the traffic as he neared Johnson.

No sooner did Johnson have him—first taking his hand, then gently seizing the thin wrist, and at last encircling the small body with his arms—than a man, the father, erupted around the corner where the dog had disappeared. Johnson inferred in an instant what must have happened. A door left carelessly ajar; the child follows the dog out of the house and the yard, then down the street, around the corner. The dog, seized by canine guilt, changes his mind and heads back home. The innocent child is abandoned to the traffic or—as it would now seem—the quivering arms of the fat old child molester.

The father and then, a moment later, the frantic mother along with the dog ran toward the boy, shouting, Never, never do that again. By the time they reached him—Johnson on his knees had the boy clamped immovable in his grip—the child was howling with fear, and Johnson found himself trying to calm them all, saying, Now, now, to the child, they're just scared, saying, Please be quiet, to the parents, I think he's very frightened. Ruff sat three yards away, thumping his tail cautiously, a little shamefaced, a little uneasy. Mother and child reunited, the father going through his stammering, inadequate thanks, Johnson found himself trying to explain that his own son had died, had run out into the street after a ball and been hit by a car, but he was crying too hard to make himself understood. A good if little-known poet, kneeling on the sidewalk, crying uncontrollably, streams of tears and snot and unintelligible words issuing from his fat red face as all four—father, mother, child, dog—stared at him with pity and unutterable embarrassment.

Soon, however, Johnson was able to get back into his car and drive home, once again destroyed by what he could never change, never forget, never explain: the death of his son. And, then, the worst event of the entire day: When he got home, he went straight to his desk and wrote it all down into a poem. Up to this point in its narrative, the poem went smoothly. Johnson knew it was by far the most rhythmic, moving, beautiful thing he had ever written, even though he wasn't totally pleased with the ending—which amounted to an admission that he hated himself for writing everything down again and again, cheapening the child's death. As it stood, the poem seemed to be saying, If you want to be a good poet, you must stop exploiting the major event of your life or the subject will come home to haunt you. This Johnson found hard to bear.

The first two times he read the poem aloud, it won a tremendous response from the audience. Not applause but deep silence broken only by the sobs of a few listeners, not poetry lovers, Johnson suspected, but fellow poets who felt the terror of the poem's message. He was reading to fairly large audiences at formal readings so that after a few moments of silence he could go on to some other poems, and this determined performance somehow contradicted the gloomy, even nihilistic advice. The third time, however, he read the poem at an informal student-faculty gathering. Twenty people—mostly students—sitting in a circle in a deserted classroom on a Friday afternoon, reciting either their own poems or those of poets whom they particularly admired. One kid had memorized "Prufrock," and after that, Johnson read the poem. The department chairman—there to give benign approval and recite some Wordsworth—broke into tears. Everyone else sat in stunned silence until a junior English major, wearing a Che Guevara tee-shirt and black-and-white-checked Vans, stood up in desperation and recited "Gunga Din": "You're a better man than I am, Gunga Din."

After this, Johnson began to tinker with the poem. At first he thought there was a problem of some sort with the rhythm of the final lines, so he changed words and then changed them back again, reversed lines, removed others, and generally moused around in a way familiar to all writers. Eventually he concluded that there was something wrong with what the poem was saying. Over a period of months, Johnson worked on the ending of the poem. He wrote fifteen final versions, each eventually discarded in favor of the next. Finally, on the sixteenth try, it was done at last. He read it through and was thoroughly satisfied. He sent it off to the *New Yorker,* which rejected it immediately, but a solidly competent academic journal accepted it, and finally reading the poem in print, Johnson knew that it was his masterpiece.

By this time, Johnson had gotten the end of the poem to say that even though he was disgusted on this specific occasion, it was really a good idea to write about his son's death because this was the subject life had given him and it was his duty to bear the burden of his life's work. A third, maybe half, of Johnson's new poems made reference to his son's death, his daughters' unhappiness, his divorce, his remarriage, and—eventually—his second divorce and the problems of moving out on his own at fifty. The poems continued to be musical and limpid, perfect for reading out loud with the force of Johnson's personality and the beauty of his voice to lend them resonance. Read to oneself, they were a shade less satisfactory, although good nevertheless, and he began to close his readings with the poem about the blond child by the side of the road and his realization that life had given him this burden to write about. Since so many of the preceding poems had been about his son's death, this poem—read at the end of the evening—began to sound unpleasantly defensive to everyone but Johnson.

*

The Lawrences had never forged neighborly ties with the World Bank couple in the adjacent row house because they resented their subsidized three percent mortgage. The Lawrences made no bones about this resentment because on principle they disapproved of the rising property values that were driving lower-middle-class blacks out of the neighborhood and turning Mount Pleasant into a place where rich people's townhouses stood cheek by jowl with tenements full of illegal aliens, like a comic-book visualization of Marxism.

The Lawrences were not Marxists or even socialists, their behavior stemming from beliefs that lacked the necessary coherence of ideology. Still, forgoing better job offers, John taught remedial science at the University of the District of Columbia, while Louise, with a first-rate law degree, stayed home to raise Emily and William, tutor black children, write occasional articles about the inequities of the tax system, and serve on dozens of neighborhood committees. Emily and William never ate candy or anything from McDonald's; they watched television on an antique black-and-white set and only the news at that; they never played with toy guns and soldiers; they had no pets because of the hair.

Louise's friends tended to be political allies rather than emotional ties. Her aloofness was certainly in force with the World Bank neighbors. She never knew anything about them beyond their three percent mortgage, and when the Mayflower van removed them to an expensive subdivision in McLean, she awaited the new owners with curiosity rather than anticipation. Louise watched the arrival of Mr. Greenpants, then observed him as he stood on his front porch, smoking steadily and contemplating the ivy, into which he tossed the butt of his old cigarette after using it to light his new. This was not a gesture she approved of, nor did she admire his bright-green corduroy trousers, a fresh shade inappropriate to anyone but a small child and particularly unsuited to Mr. Greenpants's overhanging paunch. She disliked him on the spot. He was the sort who might paint his brick façade red or tear down his front porch or remove his shutters. She could tell at a glance that he was someone who failed to understand the essential morality of living beneath your means. A day passed and then another, and Mr. Greenpants's side of the wall was as quiet as the grave. And then, an odor.

At first it was so faint that Louise didn't trust her own nose. She was baking cookies for Emily's school fair, and even though she knew it wasn't the smell of cookies, she checked the oven. Then she ran down to the basement to check the furnace and the flickering pilot light of the water heater. Then she went into every room of the house, peering into closets, opening built-in cupboards, checking for the smoke from electrical fires, and, satisfied at last, chalked it up to simple paranoia. The same quality that made her a perfectionist as a student, a mother, a housekeeper had also given her a sensitive nose. She considered this, as from a great distance, and a dark thought boiled up from nowhere: She was a perfectionist whose real, adult work did not amount to a thing. Her perfectionism was all that of preparation and in fruition amounted to nothing at all. This thought was so unexpected and so insistent that she baked several dozen more cookies trying to forget it. The extra cookies came in handy the next day when the odor returned. A strangely familiar smell, it reminded her of suffering laboratory animals, of meatpacking houses, of concentration camps, and then the mystery slowly resolved itself into the unmistakable smell of cigarette smoke coming from the wall that they shared with Mr. Greenpants.

Assuming that he would not be home, Louise packed an old Christmas tin (Currier & Ives, clean snow, fresh air) with cookies, wrote a note about the smell, and left this on Mr. Greenpants's front porch. She noted that his walk was already overhung with weeds and his porch swing was hanging by one hook. Perhaps he drank as well. What if he passed out while smoking in bed? The next morning she found the empty tin on her doorstep with a note of thanks. His name was Johnson, and he gave his telephone number; he said he was sorry about the smell. Louise assumed that it would disappear. Two days later, however, it was just as strong as ever. Louise decided to telephone. "You do understand," she explained, "that we have two small children over here."

"Well, yes, I do. And I know I smoke a great deal more than's good for me, but I don't suppose you're suggesting I give it up?"

He sounded quite pleasant, as if he were really totally in sympathy with her, and she could hardly say yes to that rhetorical question, so said no and immediately thought that he did have his nerve! She had pointed out a simple problem, and he had tricked her with words. She went on to propose that he try to smoke on the other side of his house, the one nearest old Mrs. Burdeck. Or try confining his habit to one space, the bathroom perhaps.

Johnson greeted these suggestions with laughter—he seemed the most genial of men—and said that he was willing to see if there was some channel through which the smoke—or the odor of the smoke— seeped from his house to hers, but really he didn't see himself hugging his eastern wall or cowering in the bathroom. His tone almost suggested that he would next say, I'm a grown man and this is my house and I'll smoke wherever I damn well please. But he did not say this, and their conversation closed on a tenuously pleasant tone, he suppressing his irritation, she her sense of justice. She realized that she sounded foolish, even though she was right.

Over the next week, Louise had encounters with a carpenter, a bricklayer, an air-conditioning man, even a plumber, who probed and tapped, moved furniture, left dirty marks on the walls, and failed to find the houses anything but completely isolated from each other. There was simply no connection between the two, yet the odor grew stronger every day, and one afternoon Louise was sure that she could actually see motes and currents of real smoke in the hot streak of sunshine that pried through the living-room drapes. The one thing she didn't see was Johnson himself, a man of such confirmed nocturnal habits that aside from Louise's first glimpse, no one in the family had ever laid eyes on him.

She recognized that in a sense she was disgracing herself in leaving the electrical deodorizing contraption on his doorstep, along with a pamphlet from Smoke Enders and a dozen chocolate-chip cookies. Nevertheless, she felt justified when he returned the room deodorizer to her doorstep, along with the empty plate, in sending him a clipping from the *Post* to the effect that smoking is now considered so thoroughly a behavior of the uneducated urban poor that tobacco companies tailor their advertising to lower-class blacks. Louise realized she was assuming that Johnson was a snob and a racist and would be accordingly persuaded, but she couldn't help herself. The clipping did not reappear, only the smell.

At first Louise had merely been irritated and alarmed by the odor, but the dark thought about the failure of her perfectionism, which had arisen so spontaneously the first time she smelled the smoke, was the precursor of even darker self-perceptions. As the odor permeated her consciousness, she thought about the fact that her sister was her closest friend because they were mutually afraid and jealous of each other; she thought how her father had encouraged this by pitting them against each other while denigrating everyone else; she thought how she had spent her life making little propitiatory presents to a world she despised; she wondered if her marriage was only a necessary compromise with mediocrity so that her children could repeat the pattern her father had imposed. It also occurred to her that there was—by this time in her life—absolutely nothing she could do about any of this, nothing to do but stop thinking about it, nothing to do but get rid of the smell. And was it as bad as that? Worse! Worst of all! In the last few days, she had found herself longing to smoke a cigarette. The weakling's urge, more than the dark revelations of her self, finally drove Louise to desperate measures. She would shame Johnson into compliance with her wishes.

Near the comics and the astrology, bridge, and chess columns, the *Post* featured Jim Rupert's "Every Day." On the bright side, Rupert wrote with a hometown weekly as a model. He sent kids to camp, raised money for good causes, and fought for the underdog by using his column to embarrass evildoers. On the dimmer side, he often seemed at a loss for material and, when the well dried up, was apt to resort to personal anecdote, particularly tales of his family life, which centered on the Ruperts' only child, eight-year-old Cecelia.

William was in Cecelia's class at Beauvoir—not a public school, as the Lawrences would have preferred, but "absolutely wonderful." Although Cecelia and William were not particularly good friends, their parents met at school functions, and at one of these Louise took the bold step of telling Rupert about Johnson's smoking—making light of it, of course, treating it as if it were just one of those amusing little annoyances of everyday life that Rupert so loved to report—and like a fish to the bait, Rupert rose to half a column on the rights of nonsmokers, the ultimate victims, and specifically the poor innocent Lawrence children, William and Emily, of the nineteen-hundred block of Park Road—special friends of his little Cecelia—who were suffering from the egregious behavior of their self-indulgent neighbor, Quentin Johnson. Louise gloated over the column—read or at least scanned by everyone because of its crucial position near astrology—and expected a shamefaced apology or perhaps an outraged phone call from Johnson. What she got was more smoke.

*

It was not until a few mornings after the column appeared, just as Louise was fighting the desire to go out and buy a carton of Marlboros—her father's brand—that she finally got a relevant phone call. It was from her classmate Felicia, trying as usual to raise money for Swarthmore. An English major, Felicia had done nothing since graduation except get married, but she had the sort of belief in the value of education that made her capable of suggesting not just once but repeatedly, year after year, that whatever it was they had become, they owed it all to Swarthmore. "You met John there. You gained self-confidence—"

"I've always had self-confidence."

"If you hadn't gone to Swarthmore, you wouldn't have the nerve to browbeat that poor poet into giving up his cigarettes."

"Whatever are you talking about?" Louise was outraged—at herself—humiliated, embarrassed. She hung up on the triumphant Felicia, rushed to the Cleveland Park library, and discovered for herself that Johnson was not just any poet. He was a Yale Younger Poet! He had scores of poems published all over the place! Not that poetry should change things, Louise thought. But it did. To deny a poet his cigarettes, to shame him in print made her feel as if she were worse than Fanny Brawne and the *Edinburgh Review* rolled into one. She saw herself as unspeakable, and indeed, she realized that however she apologized—which she must quickly do—she could not do it face to face in words. Being abject wasn't in her nature. She must find some dignified way. A cake immediately suggested itself. He seemed to like chocolate, so chocolate it would be. Dark and gooey, many layered. Louise devoted all afternoon to devising this delectable apology until it occurred to her that baking a cake was a typical reaction on her part and hardly adequate for the occasion. Suddenly disgusted with herself, she set the cake aside and decided instead to write an apology in Johnson's chosen form.

Although Louise had never written a poem, she had always excelled at everything to do with language. She found her old high

19

school English survey text, refreshed her mind as to the requirements of the sonnet, and found that writing a sonnet wasn't all that easy. At first, she thought she might prefer the Italian to the English and envisioned in the eight/six line division a symbolic statement about smoking: more going in than coming out—tar, nicotine. . . . But putting this down in words was beyond her, and besides, it was too cute. At four o'clock the carpool arrived, and William discovered her sitting at the kitchen table staring at her cake in defeat.

He himself was very happy. Like all good elementary schools, Beauvoir encouraged its students to express themselves creatively with the assumption that the poetic impulse flowers in the meanest child, and that day every student in Mrs. Dugan's class had made a kite—complete with tail—onto which was pasted a poem of the child's own devising. "Mrs. Dugan says I have real talent," William boasted. "Mine was the best in the class."

"I'm sure it was!" Louise replied, reading over the poem, inspired with a new idea. "You know what would be nice? Why don't you take your kite next door and give it to Mr. Johnson? He's a poet too, so I'm sure he'll appreciate it."

William's kite featured an abstract design of brilliant tropical fish. His poem was perhaps more musical than metrical.

Flying high,
Flying low,
Oh, wind, please blow.
Red, gold, purple, green.
My, that wind sure is mean.
I just stand there watching it blow,
Telling my kite to go, go, go.
Flying high,
Gliding low,
Oh, wind, please blow.

Louise knew that this was an apology any poet would cherish.

*

We will never know what Johnson thought in those last moments when he opened his front door to find a blond eight-year-old boy holding a kite and reciting a poem about the wind, for he died almost immediately of a heart attack. The day must have grown dark around him, closing in with a rush of wings that echoed the dark voice within, the voice he had denied: Stay away from your life or it will come back to haunt you. Or the doorbell might have announced the ultimate confirmation: His poetry was a true success, for at last it had summoned up the child who had died.

As for William, there's no denying it's marked him for life, the dying poet reaching out to claim him for his own. Although in therapy and doing well, he remains withdrawn and moody, fond of words, frequently boastful, given to taking his psychic pulse and finding in it the heartbeat of the world.

Judas and the Slave Girl

When I was thirteen, I was in love with a man exactly three times my age. This year he would have been ninety-nine, if he'd lived.

No Mason of high degree could have put greater faith in numbers than I did at the time: 13:39. I actually fell in love with him when I was twelve, but I knew that when I turned thirteen, he would love me back. To put my story in the nutshell from which I shall subsequently extract it, I belonged to a children's theater group, and the man I loved conducted his dance classes—tap, ballet, and modern—in the studio next door. He had recently returned from out West to the birthplace he had left when he was eighteen. Although he'd planned on becoming a movie star, he was now a student at the local teachers' college, Ball State.

I think he came home to forge a realistic career for himself in middle age, but I really don't know. A child in love has so few ways of gathering information and even less right than usual to question the beloved, who enjoys a real difference in status, not just the difference imagined by all lovers. I don't know why Richard came back. I don't know what he did for the twenty-one years he was away. At the time I could only vaguely imagine him out in Hollywood, not as a successful actor, of course, but as a glamorous failure. For the most part, I looked into his mysterious past as if it were a crystal ball in which coagulated rich, albeit murky, images of life far, far away from Muncie, Indiana.

I am trying to avoid names in this story, but my own bears the same numerical relationship to "Dora" as "Muncie" does to "Vienna," and as for the man I loved, I'll call him Richard.

*

I have always been reluctant to tell this story, initially, I think, because I was afraid it would somehow make me seem strange—if it didn't, conversely, make me seem downright ordinary. This confusion I drank in with the water and breathed in with the air of the town I grew up in, for typicality might be thought rare and precious, so assiduously has it been sought in the environs of Muncie. In the twenties and thirties, Helen and Robert Lynd chose the town for their pioneering sociological works, *Middletown* (1929) and *Middletown in Transition* (1937). Then, in the seventies and eighties, scholars at the University of Virginia chose to replicate and expand the Lynds' work. It was only after coming across one of these books, *Middletown Families,* that I began to wonder whether the story of that Easter morning in the 1950s was far from commonplace, although not particularly strange.

When I imagine the Muncie I grew up in, I take a bird's-eye view: The White River undulates back on itself, a thin brown snake trying to swallow its tail as it catches in its coils a small, innocent place utterly uninterested in self-knowledge and consumed by the need to keep up a good front. What strong local pride! Certainly I was not the only creature in Muncie who confused the typical with the ordinary and invested it with a dimension of scorn. How boring it is—how truly boring!—to be the norm. You may suspect that you are ordinary, but who wants to know? Who wants others to know? Like most of the characters in this story, I lived in hysterical avoidance of the normal, that is, when I didn't live in fear of seeming strange.

Not surprisingly, life in Muncie in the 1950s was characterized by a high degree of standardization. The town was surrounded by fields of soybeans and corn, row after row after row of them. The principal industry was the manufacture of automotive parts, the production line the destiny of most of its inhabitants. The Lynds accurately posited the existence of two basic classes—white-collar business (who lived on the north side of town) and blue-collar labor (who lived on the south side)—but both groups were marked by highly cherished inner differences, features of a powerful desire for distinction that the Lynds underestimated. For example, the Green Hills Country Club and the Delaware Country Club, nearly identical to the outside eye, saw themselves as harboring vastly different memberships. Similarly, the working class belonged to organizations whose very appellations baffle the foreigner: How can you tell a Moose from an Elk? an Odd Fellow from a Mason? or, for that matter, a Baptist from a Methodist? Typically, the earliest and strongest of my own conscious desires was to belong to something that would distinguish me from everyone else.

My parents were originally from the southern part of the state and well along in life when they moved to Muncie. They were isolated both as newcomers and as nonchurchgoers in a uniformly Christian community, but, above all, they were simply not joiners; my father preferred an angry loneliness that veered off into obsessive pursuits (swimming long distances), while my mother, suffering from feelings of social inferiority, suspected all her acquaintances of snubbing her and paid them back in kind. For me, an only child, another isolating factor was that I was perceived as being unusually bright. To my father, I had a tremendous potential that he knew I would never live up to. To my mother, I was Seven Sisters material right from the start. These notions were rigidified by that normative invention, the standardized I.Q. test, which, thanks to the nearby teachers' college, was a recurring feature of our lives. Of course, when my horizons expanded, I discovered that I really wasn't all that bright, but back then, my Stanford-Binet score signed me clearly with the mark of Cain. I was one of Muncie's oddities along with the physically deformed, the chemically mad, homosexuals, and political radicals. In short, I was obsessed, early on, with the fear that I would never belong, even while I was securely grouped with a collection of outcasts. Not long ago I came across a photograph neatly sissored from the *Muncie Evening Star* that showed me as a fierce tiger in *Little Black Sambo*. There I was, clad in striped long underwear, roaring my way around an ersatz palm tree. Soon a piece of yellow canvas would drop from the sky and magically turn me into butter. I said in the first paragraph of this story that I "belonged" to a children's theater, but really it was far more than that. What I belonged to was Isabella Anderson's Children's Playhouse, located on the third floor of the Commercial Building on Main Street in downtown Muncie, Indiana.

*

When I was growing up, buildings in Muncie said what they meant. For example, the Field House, home of the Muncie Central Bearcats, who had won more state basketball championships than any other team in Indiana, was the biggest building in town. Similarly, the Masonic Temple was Muncie's tallest, most spiritual edifice. Churches, banks, and the mansions of industrial magnates were built either of imperishable stone that looked as if it had been looted from Roman ruins or colonial-style brick no wolf could ever blow in. Neon signs correctly labeled bars and movie theaters. Ordinary houses were small, white, and set in lots shaded by strangely productive trees like mulberries and catalpas. Only age and the tricks of fortune taught these structures to speak with more than one voice.

The three-story Commercial Building was eloquent in its way. Its classical embellishment whispered of high aspirations, but even though it sat on Main Street, the real business district had long ago moved to North Walnut and left the building stranded in the backwater of its ambitions, a jumble of auto-supply shops and cheap bars that spoke of simple failure. The principal tenant of the Commercial Building, the Gas Company, had replaced much of the first-floor facade with plate glass in order to show off appliances that looked like white-enameled ice cubes dumped from the inverted trays of the embossed metal ceiling. With a captive clientele, the Gas Company cared little about location. Equally indifferent were the renters of the second floor, the Muncie Chamber of Commerce. Theirs was a dark space furnished with red leatherette chairs facing each other at nonintersecting angles as if recently vacated by people with nothing in common. It was an enterprise that despaired of any information sufficiently interesting to lure a stranger up off the street. At one side of the room, a broad, comfortable staircase climbed its way to the cheap third floor and Children's Playhouse.

Although details flood my memory, the general impression was one of dusty clutter and flagrant theatricality. Isabella had chosen a color scheme of pink and green, perhaps to connote comedy and tragedy, while the paired faces—mouth up, mouth down—provided a pervasive decorative motif. The main room featured a lot of mirrors, a piano, a barre, and, at one end, a stage—built by Isabella's husband, Bill, a fireman in real life, a set designer in the world of Children's

Playhouse. In addition, there were a large reception room, a storage room for props and costumes, and several smaller cubbyholes, one of which had been converted to a dance studio by Richard when he came back from out West.

Isabella herself was a faded beauty. Originally a blonde, she began to bleach her hair once it turned white, a double gilding of the lily that represented her attitude toward life. Bosomy, she sometimes wore falsies; tiny, she either teetered on spike heels or slithered around in ballet slippers. Sometimes I thought she was beautiful, sometimes ugly as sin, but always, always glamorous. When Isabella was twenty, she had intended to go to New York City to become an actress but had gotten pregnant and married Bill instead. Testimony to her powerful personality, this shotgun wedding only added to her stature in the community, and her disappointed intention of going to New York still served her legend thirty-five years later.

At the time, I considered knowing her the greatest good fortune of my life.

*

When I was seven or so, at what must have been a substantial expense for them at the time, my parents enrolled me in Children's Playhouse. Every week, I spent an hour with a group of children my age, learning to be things other than what we were. Isabella made no effort to render these lessons age-appropriate. Instead, we were treated as if, though young in years, we too appreciated life's tragic workings, the stuff equally of myth and gossip, the essence of reality.

Most of Isabella's instruction consisted of telling us stories that we then acted out up on the stage. Some of these stories—"The Monkey's Paw," for example—were clearly fiction because Isabella held on to a book while she told them. Others were not fiction because Isabella related them to us as the truth. My favorite—told time after time—concerned a bank teller, Joe, from a little crossroads village over near Yorktown, happily married and father of a newborn son. Falling behind in his work, Joe brings several thousand dollars of the bank's money home with him one night in order to count it. He stands at his desk near the fireplace, tearing the paper bands off the packets and throwing them into the flames to the delight of his wife's brother, a moron, who loves to watch the fire. Just when Joe has finished counting the money, he is called by his wife (Maria) to come admire the baby, who splashes in the tub. Joe grinds out his cigarette (no smoke for his baby!) and hurries off, whereupon the moronic brother starts tossing the money into the fire to watch it burn with the same beautiful glow as the bands. Just as the last bills are tossed onto the fire, Joe returns and rushes to save what he can from the blaze. In so doing, he knocks over Maria's brother, who hits his head on the fender. Frightened by the sound, Maria rushes in, finds her brother with his head all bloody (in fact, he is dead), and rushes back to the bathroom for some water to revive him. And then from off-stage comes a heartrending scream. The darling baby has drowned in the bathtub.

This anecdote so inspired me at the time that my spirit soared high above the town I lived in, beyond its neat square blocks of commercial intent, into the empyrean overview of tragedy. Up on Isabella's stage I loved to pretend that I was Joe, or Maria, or even the moronic brother. How surprised I was in later life to come across this story in Constantin Stanislavsky's *An Actor Prepares*. Joe's name is Kostya, Vanya the name of the moronic brother, Maria is Maria still. "From the other room a heartrending scream is heard. The darling baby is dead—drowned in its bath." If I'd known this at the time, what would have shocked (and pleased) me most was the Russian origin of this appealing fable. It was the fifties, remember, and Muncie was on the front lines of that propaganda battle known as the Cold War. It may well have been that Isabella disguised the source of her story in order to conceal its enemy origins.

For years, not unlike the moronic brother, I basked in the devouring glow of my weekly drama lesson, which was, however, not entirely devoted to sending reality up in smoke. We also learned useful tips for everyday life: how to sit down without looking back at the chair (feel the edge of the seat with the back of your knees); how to sit properly (knees together, lower legs slanted off to the side); how to walk down stairs without looking at your feet (forgotten); how to pronounce "doesn't" ("duznt," not "duddnt"), "newspaper" ("nieus paper," not "noose paper"), and "Washington" ("Wasssshington," not "Warrrshington"); how to say "What?," not "Huh?," "Yes," not "Yeah," and "Hello," not "Pleastamecha"; how to thank people for gifts and favors ("Thank you"); how to express grief at deaths and other misfortunes

("I'm sorry"); and how to correctly introduce people of various ages, sexes, and degrees. (How difficult to figure this out even though we lived in a Midwestern democracy!) Isabella advised us to keep it simple and have faith in our instincts.

At the real heart of the enterprise, Isabella annually put on three full-scale productions for a local audience—either fairy tales (*Little Red Riding Hood, Hansel and Gretel, Snow White and the Seven Dwarfs*) or children's stories (*Heidi, Robin Hood, King Midas and the Golden Touch*). I think these plays must have been published by some association founded to promote children's theater; I will never forget their pale-blue paper covers. Every child cast in a speaking part was given a clean new script; then, for several months, we rehearsed the play twice a week after school until a final dress rehearsal was followed by three performances (Friday and Saturday nights and Saturday afternoon) on the stage of the Muncie Central High School auditorium. Then we threw away the dog-eared, underlined, food-stained, finger-grubbed scripts and moved eagerly on to the next play: casting, reading through, blocking, and rehearsal after rehearsal after rehearsal until we once again reached those exciting occasions of nervous stomachs, greasepaint, lush costumes, glaring lights, and flimsy sets (so unconvincing up close and probably from far away too). And then on to the third play. This comforting pattern lent relief to the boredom of school and the restraints of parents, who were allowed to come only to the dress rehearsals and the actual performances.

My own didn't even do that. My mother explained to me right at the beginning, when I was a little fairy in *Sleeping Beauty*, that the mothers and fathers of professional actresses never attend their children's performances, which are, after all, simply part of the job. Thereafter, I took pride in complete parental absence. And so it was with most of the children who frequented Children's Playhouse. We were left alone to exercise our considerable imaginations in what our parents must have considered a benign atmosphere of cultural enrichment.

Our performances were to full houses. Probably every child in Muncie went to at least one play a year. Indeed, many "normal" children were sent by their parents for a year or two of Children's Playhouse lessons, which were reputed to encourage a cheerful poise, a bland grace. Nevertheless, by the time they were eleven or so, these children, as well as their parents, had generally had enough of Children's Playhouse. It was acting in the plays year after year after year—long after we'd stopped taking lessons—that marked some of us as "belonging." And after testing our wings at Children's Playhouse, we graduated to the Muncie Civic Theatre and Ball State's Shoestring Theatre so that, having cast our lot with Children's Playhouse, we eventually found ourselves belonging to a countywide—even a state-wide—society of oddballs.

While I am still at a distance from the story toward which I creep, I will describe a few of the children who truly "belonged" to Children's Playhouse, that is, who stayed on for years acting in Isabella's plays and experiencing the larger theatrical scene. There was Sonny, my age, who resembled a myopic praying mantis. When he was a year old, his mother had painted his finger- and toenails red and, carrying him up to the altar at St. Lawrence's, dedicated him to the Virgin Mary. Years later it occurred to me that Sonny was a hermaphrodite, probably not a common problem in Muncie and one his mother faced with intelligence and grace. I'm told that in his twenties he was in the chorus line of a few Broadway productions and had begun to make a name for himself in costume design when he was killed in an automobile accident. There were the pudgy twins, Karen and Sharen, always ready to go along—although slowly—as if each had only half a personality and less than half a brain. They grew up to be cardiac nurses and were unusually fertile, getting their names in the paper when they each gave birth to a set of twins. There was Clarissa. Poor and aspiring, three or four years older than the rest of us, and the oldest of eleven casually neglected children, she worked for Isabella as a paid assistant, wild to bring order into all our lives. Following her advice on pimples left me ever so slightly scarred for life. My favorite was Bobbie, who fearlessly bleached his hair and wore mascara. Everyone knew he'd be a star, and, sure enough! he ended up teaching drama at a university in Texas until he died of AIDS in the 1980s.

While I considered myself superior to Clarissa and equal to Sonny, the twins, and even Bobbie, my relationship with Maggi was that of a human being to whom every now and then a goddess condescends. The year I was twelve and then thirteen, Maggi—or more precisely Maggi with a little balloon dotting the i and lifting her high above all the Margarets she'd grown up with—was sixteen and then seventeen. She'd graduated from some deficient high school out in the county and was working at a jewelry store to save up enough money to go to New York City and become an actress. A fragile elf, what else could she be, with her dead white skin, black, curly hair, and violet eyes? Utterly plain, I admired her so much because I knew I could never be like her. Maggi was also in love with Richard, and he was in love with her.

*

At the time I fell in love with Richard, I considered myself by no means innocent. I knew that homosexuality, adultery, and incest were natural because through my involvement with community theater, I already knew quite a number of homosexuals and adulterers, plus one set of grown-up twins who—according to Clarissa—regularly had sexual intercourse with each other. Literature confirmed experience: I had encountered adultery in *Anna Karenina*, although I knew that anything the Russians did ceased to be ordinary. The opposite of us, they brought to all occasions a rarefying passion. What I didn't understand were the mechanical specifics of even heterosexual sex. I was not too clear about sperm and ejaculation, and I was totally in the dark about erections. From the statues I'd seen, everything seemed headed in the wrong direction. I don't want to suggest that I brooded about this. That September I had set about reading my way through the Great Books, which I can still see lined up in their prim covers on a shelf in the adult room of the Muncie Public Library. I found them rough going, but given enough time and patience, I knew that I was certain to master them thoroughly. And just as I cheerfully jumped over words I didn't understand and guiltlessly skipped whole paragraphs full of meaningless prose, so I thought of sex as a page full of blanks that would eventually fill themselves in. I mention this to put quotation marks around the phrase "in love with" Richard.

*

Although Richard arrived on the scene in September, I did not fall in love with him immediately. I still found him uninteresting in October, when Clarissa told me about his affair with Maggi. It was not until

31

November, when the Muncie Civic Theatre put on its first production of the season, that I too fell in love.

Civic staged its productions in the auditorium of the Masonic Temple, a real theater with a box office, plush seats, crystal chandeliers, maroon velvet curtains, and bona fide dressing rooms. Even after I grew familiar with this auditorium, I could never take it for granted because of the building in which it was lodged. The designation of "temple" marked it as holy space and dangerous ground. Never will I forget my state of dizzy receptivity on that cold fall night when my parents dropped me off at the Masonic Temple for Civic's production of *Anastasia*.

The plot was simple, the implications remarkably gratifying. It is Berlin 1926, and Prince Bounine is perpetrating a swindle. To a group of investors, he will produce Princess Anastasia Nicolaevna Romanov, not killed with her family in the cellar at Ekaterinburg but alive and ready to claim the ten million pounds that Tsar Nicholas deposited in Swiss banks before the Revolution. The investors—and Prince Bounine—will be rich. Anna, the girl Bounine has found to impersonate Anastasia, turns out, however, to actually *be* the princess, and she is recognized as such by her grandmother, the Dowager Empress. Anastasia then grows disgusted with the greed of Prince Bounine, as well as with his continuing disbelief in her identity, and so, with the Dowager Empress's blessing, she runs away to live her own life, knowing who she really is and convinced—as the White Russians are not—that the past is the past and, hence, irrecoverable. Bounine is left with his ruined scheme, defeated either by the royal tradition (as the Dowager Empress would have it) or by the mad Romanovs (as he himself believes).

A wonderful play filled with recognition scenes that happily define that elusive trait, true nobility! Bounine, although thoroughly aristocratic, is a scoundrel, while Anastasia, the presumed imposter, is the real thing because she abandons the romanticized past, scorns ostentatious wealth, and accepts her true self through her grandmother's love. Love! the real meaning of family relationships, not mere genealogical succession!

For weeks after seeing the play, I found myself imagining that Anastasia had a daughter, a lost and then rediscovered daughter. Me! My superiority was thus confirmed by my identity, an inherent worth enhanced by undeserved suffering. People fell at my feet; I graciously raised them up, knowing who I really was—a real princess. And Russian too! On more sensible days, I believed that nobility lies within everybody's reach. Give up demeaning romanticism! Don't be greedy! Know—and be—thyself! Love others! The first fantasy was, of course, by far the more compelling. Yet I'm not sure the play would have affected me half so intensely had I not known the actors. What would *Anastasia* have been without Isabella as the strong-willed Dowager Empress, Maggi as the genuine Anastasia, and Richard as the evil Prince Bounine? Watching this cast, I saw with the piercing inaccuracy of the preadolescent heart that the various notions of nobility designated by the play were actually embodied in the people acting out the roles.

Far and away the best scene was Isabella's recognition of Maggi as her granddaughter, although Maggi's recognition of herself as a valid person and Richard's recognition of defeat were splendid too. I can still see Isabella as the "small but straight-backed and indomitable" Empress, who suggests to Anastasia that they run away together to her "old palace in Finland." In watching this scene, I saw how superior Isabella was to Muncie and how she was really looking for a spiritual granddaughter to carry on Children's Playhouse after her death. I did not see the irony of Isabella's life, lived in a town without history, superimposed on the Empress's royal past. Nor did I think of Isabella's two daughters and five grandchildren. And what of Maggi? I no doubt caught her resemblance to the unrecognized but true princess. As for any dissimilarity—even to my eye Maggi was not quite the real thing, given any accepted definition of "real"—I admired her too much to admit her falseness. And Richard? For reasons I didn't understand, his attraction lay in his similarity to an aristocratic knave. Even though I knew Richard was made of finer clay than other men, he was by no means an aristocrat even by my limited standards, and while he was attractive because he seemed somehow "bad," I knew of no specific crime he had committed. And yet the converse—that he was a sterling example of everyday respectability—seemed unthinkable.

Layers and layers pierced with the unifying vision of the almost innocent. It now seems impossible that I saw them in this way because I now know that Isabella had a stroke that left her paralyzed for the last twenty years of her life; that no one stepped in to take over Children's Playhouse; that Maggi did indeed go to New York City but in no guise that fulfilled her ambitions; and that Richard received his degree from Ball State with a major in English and, after teaching junior high school for a number of years, dropped dead in his late forties from a heart attack.

*

Having seen Anastasia, I easily understood why Richard and Maggi had fallen in love with each other. I was not at all jealous. I knew that at twelve I was still too young. Nevertheless, I awaited my teenage years confidently, my love for Richard growing stronger by the day.

That year, Isabella's first production was *Little Black Sambo*. Then, in December, we went into rehearsal for *Cinderella*. Richard was the Prince's father; Maggi was Cinderella's stepmother; I, an ugly stepsister, a role I played with the gusto of magical thinking: Maybe if I acknowledged the truth, it would not be true. Although the three of us were in a sense united by our secondary roles, the play was not very exciting for me because Richard and Maggi only attended an occasional Saturday rehearsal. Left on my own, I joined Sonny and the twins in experimenting with a Ouija board, Tarot cards, and (aided by a candle) hypnosis. I decided to give up on the Great Books and instead read Dostoevsky, delighted to discover that Richard had read him too, as he told me one day when he found me huddled over my book in the makeshift dressing room at Children's Playhouse. Confused as I sometimes was by the life around me, I knew Dostoevsky was the real thing, and I announced to Richard that I was going to be a famous novelist when I grew up. I don't recall that he laughed at my announcement. What wonderful conversations we had about Dostoevsky and Tolstoy and even Gogol. Too bad I'd never heard of Nabokov.

At first, I paid no heed to the rumors—conveyed by Clarissa—that Maggi's parents strongly opposed her involvement with Richard. Clarissa could not understand why. I, however, began to sense a reason for parental concern. Perhaps it was during one of our discussions that I noticed a peculiar odor hanging about Richard, which I finally recognized as that of liquor. Since I knew absolutely nothing about alcoholism (my parents were abstainers), I don't know how I derived so many explanations from this whiff of information, but by the time

Maggi and Richard gave me their photographs, I firmly associated Richard's suffering yet somehow malignant intelligence with drink. No wonder Maggie's parents disapproved of him! No wonder he was at loose ends at thirty-nine! No wonder he was so old! For if at first I had thought Richard was old *because* he was thirty-nine, I now began to suspect (as I slowly approached thirteen) that he was old *for* thirty-nine.

Those photographs! In my memory, Maggi's face still has a matte surface, slightly blurred features, and dewy eyes. Her photograph was only two by three inches, so her handwriting on the back was less circular than usual. The cramped inscription said, in gold ink, that mine was the face of a great portrait. I took this to be a kind way of telling me I wasn't pretty.

Much as I cherished Maggi's photograph, it was mere wastepaper compared to Richard's glossy eight-by-eleven-inch publicity still. As if emerging from deep shadows, Richard looked down at the lower right-hand corner from a brooding angle that emphasized his hooded eyes and the thin bitterness of his lips, which nightly I kissed ever so carefully in order to leave no smudges on their shining surface. Then I imagined him seated alone at a plain wooden table, hunched over a glass, staring down at a bottle, a cigarette wreathing up clouds of inspirational smoke: a seer suffering the pain of his knowledge. Now I see a hawk painfully digesting a tough morsel. I wish I could recall the scene in which he gave me his photograph. With adult knowledge that memory would establish many things. But alas! I have forgotten, or perhaps there was no scene to remember. Perhaps Maggi simply gave me Richard's photograph along with her own. As you have no doubt noticed, I cannot tell this story in "scenes." This is because I can recall very few that took place in "real" life, although I can vividly remember the scenes we played on stage.

Cinderella passed like a dream. During my daytime hours, I alternated between concerns about my body and fantasies about Richard. Glass slippers were in the air, and my worries focused on the size of my feet. If only I could wear ballet slippers for everyday and spike heels for special occasions, my problems would be solved because, to my mind, the former compressed your foot, while the latter set the inordinate length of your foot on an incline that shortened the distance on the ground from heel to toe. In my nighttime fantasies, a slightly drunk Richard knelt unsteadily at my tiny high-heeled feet telling me that, despite my age, I knew a lot about the tragic nature of life and he could hardly wait until I turned thirteen.

＊

Here is a scene from "real" life that came back to me recently. My classmate Moira actually hated Richard. She took private tap classes from him, and she was dying to stop. She claimed Richard was too bossy. Since her parents doted on her younger sister and Moira was frequently in trouble with teachers as well as other authority figures, I figured that her dislike of Richard was just one more instance of rebellion. Then, early one Saturday morning before anyone but Clarissa was around, I found Moira all but bursting with rage at something Richard had made her do at her lesson the afternoon before. Strangling on unspoken words, Moira pulled me back to the small room where Richard taught. It was a nice room. He had painted the walls white and refinished the floors himself, sanding and varnishing them until they shone like a basketball court. No one was around, not even Clarissa. Moira drew me inside and shut the door. We observed his room, Moira in a furious, I in a worshipping silence until she took a lipstick out of her pocket and began writing bright-red words all over the white walls: FUCK, SHIT, and so forth. An emotion too big for her body compelled the lipstick across the wall.

As soon as I caught my breath, I ran away. Later that day, when Isabella questioned everyone about the vandalism, I held my tongue. I did not lie so much as I simply chose to forget the scene I had witnessed. I had always believed that insanity must be interesting because it was different from being normal, but Moira was not interesting. She was terrifying, and I was left without words to expose her. As it turned out, my silence amounted to little, because Richard just repainted his walls and Moira stopped taking tap classes. I understand that when she grew up she was an organizer for the UAW and ended up with thirty-six grandchildren, something of a record in these days of zero population growth.

＊

Muncie was—and by all accounts still is—a religious community, its belief in Christ Crucified one of its most cherished notions. So what could be more sensible than a citywide reenactment of the Passion and Resurrection of Jesus in the Field House at sunrise on Easter morning? Maybe the pageant was a long-standing Munsonian tradition. I only participated in the one, and I'd like to think it was unique.

Years later in college, when we got to T. S. Eliot, I started reading the 1922 edition of *The Golden Bough* one night and couldn't put it down. In fact, just the other day, I came across my copy. If I had time I'd read it all again. Just consider these enticing items listed, among many, many others, in the index:

• Agricultural year, expulsion of demons timed to coincide with seasons of the;

• Christian festivals displace heathen festivals, see Easter;

• Easter, resemblance to the festival of, to the rites of Adonis; assimilated to the Spring festival of Attis, controversy as to origin of;

• Fires, perpetual; the Lenten; Easter; burning of men and animals in the;

• Hearts, of men eaten to acquire their qualities;

• Isis, a corn goddess; resemblance to the Virgin Mary; dirge of;

• Israelites, slaughter of firstborn by, see also Christ, Passover;

• King, the killing of the divine; his life sympathetically bound up with the prosperity of the country; sacrifice of his son;

• May Bride, May-bushes, May-pole;

• Puberty, girls secluded at; initiatory rites at;

• Resurrection, of a god in the hunting, pastoral, and agricultural stages of society; enacted in Shrove-tide and Lenten ceremonies; of the effigy of

• Death; of the Wild Man; of Attis; of Osiris, of Persephone; of Dionysus;

• Sacrifice, of king's son; of virility;

• Sacrifices, of children among the Semites;

• Sexual intercourse, practiced to make the crops and fruit grow;
• Vegetation, homeopathic influence of persons on; men and women masquerading as the spirits of; marriage of the powers of; death and revival of the spirit of; perhaps generalized from a tree-spirit; growth and decay of; decay and revival of, in the rites of Adonis; gardens of Adonis charms to promote the growth of; Attis as a god of; Osiris as a god of; decay and growth of, conceived as the death and resurrection of gods.

Of course, when I was thirteen I knew nothing about how important it was to sacrifice a human being in order to ensure the fertility of the crops. All I knew was that Isabella had been asked to direct the Easter pageant, and we all had to help because it was such a challenge. For one thing, a lot of people were involved. A surprising number of Muncie's citizens volunteered to be crucifying Jerusalemites and Roman soldiers, while so many church choirs were involved that they eventually filled the lower bleachers of the Field House. It was also a challenge because all the chief characters had been familiar to the audience from earliest childhood. Everyone had a perfectly clear idea of Jesus, the Virgin Mary, Pontius Pilate, Judas, and the rest so that Isabella's problem was to cast the parts in a way that would win the audience's agreement. Confidently she rose to the challenge.

First, Jesus. By luck, Isabella found a preacher from a small church on the south side of town, the Reverend John Dotson, Reverend Johnny as we called him. In his early thirties, about six feet tall, he sported natural Jesus Christ–blond hair. Although his church was of the tongue-speaking, snake-handling variety opposed to theatrical representations, Isabella somehow won him over.

The role of the Virgin Mary was filled by one of Isabella's close friends, a tall, pale blonde in her midthirties. A decade later, Donna's life would be shattered by tragedy when her handsome blond husband, Muncie's premier deejay, wrecked his motorcycle and was paralyzed from the neck down. But even back then Donna had an air of self-sacrifice.

For Mary Magdalene, Isabella needed someone with a spotless reputation and a dark, disturbing beauty. She luckily stumbled onto Mrs. Westlake, the wife of a popular Methodist minister.

Yet another stroke of luck. Mr. Smith, an unctuous-looking banker with a good sense of humor, volunteered himself as Pontius Pilate because, as he said, he was used to accepting what was rendered unto Caesar.

And then, best of all, eleven members of the Kiwanis Club volunteered to be the disciples. They all had sandy-brown hair, fat faces, and incipient potbellies and were as pleased with themselves as if they were actually up for sainthood. The cleverest of their number, infinitely capable of denying anything that caused trouble, was given the keys to the kingdom, but Judas was a more demanding role, and for him Isabella chose Richard himself.

With lots of spectacle-demanding time on her hands, Isabella also made a useful interpretation of the New Testament by creating a role for Maggi as the rich mistress of Pontius Pilate who is converted at the sight of Jesus entering Jerusalem. The rest of us provided suitable cosmetic touches. Karen and Sharen were Jerusalem teenagers. (They had to drop out later when their parents took them off to Florida for spring vacation.) Clarissa was Saint Anne; Sonny, a rather young Herod; and Bobbie, the most Roman of gambling soldiers. I was Maggi's glittering slave girl and would have my little moment when Jesus walked by and Maggi climbed down from her litter and renounced her wealth (me). I was particularly pleased with my part. While Maggi's role demanded talent, mine provided simple visual splendor.

The rehearsals were confused affairs at best. In a room deep inside the Masonic Temple, we stared at chalk marks on a marble floor that suggested rituals far more sumptuous than the Passion. An unused smell permeated the place, cold and metallic, like the daytime odor of a tree in which tribes of departed starlings have roosted for the night.

A lot depended on the litter—not yet built—which was clearly more important theatrically than Maggi and I. Four wrestlers from Ball State were to carry it, and it was to be preceded by several fan-bearing drama majors. During rehearsals, we clustered around its invisible dimensions, and it was during these dull vigils that I divined all was not well between Maggi and Richard. It grew increasingly clear that he was tired of her. He never came over to talk, sticking instead with his own porcine group of disciples, and Maggi sullenly indicated that she was leaving for New York City next summer, come hell or high water. Of course, I never explicitly asked her what was wrong. Although I had turned thirteen at last, she was now seventeen and still too far ahead of me for such familiarity. I was growing up, but Maggi, no longer a fragile waif, had suddenly turned into a real woman with large breasts, a big behind, and a clearly defined mission in life.

The week before Easter, we met in the Field House for more elaborate rehearsals, which were even more depressing than those held in the Masonic Temple. There, our message had merely seemed inadequate to the room; here, our very essence seemed futile, barren matter thinly stretched through empty space. By the end of March, the basketball championship tournaments were over, yet the smell of sweat lingered to tell us what Indiana audiences really believed in. The Field House even had an altar, located next to the ticket office, a case full of trophies that looked like gilded saints. Yet, one by one, clues to our purpose appeared. Bill and his crew of firemen produced a fairly solid-looking cross, a stone for the mouth of the tomb, and, best of all, a litter. What a miracle of stagecraft! Up close it looked like what it was, a frame of kindling to which Bill had nailed someone's old living-room drapes. But at a distance, what Oriental sexual perversions did that litter manage to suggest! It was as if its foursquare boxiness contained the whole world that was, symbolically, offered up by Satan to be refused by Christ and, specifically, paid for by Pontius Pilate to be abandoned by Maggi. It was an altar fit for a magnificent ritual: the cutting of Isaac's throat, the burning of a firstborn, the disembowelment of a scapegoat. Stretched on its expanse, a Virgin should have her smoking heart wrenched from her chest by the bloody hands of the Feathered God.

Gradually the dispirited people around us also began to gather meaning as they acquired shreds of costume. A black shawl created a peasant, a helmet a soldier, a robe a disciple, wings an angel. Gradually we made ready for the dress rehearsal. There would be a Crucifixion and a Resurrection after all, although, of course, both of those events would take place offstage. Everybody understood that theater just wasn't up to that. In the pageant we would simply enact the surrounding scenes.

Isabella realized that she had far too many citizens on her hands for a proper dress rehearsal, and so, at eight o'clock on the night of Holy Saturday, the united choirs assembled for their final run-through. When they finished, they were free to go home until the next morning, when they would show up for the performance. Our rehearsal did not begin until eleven; after that, wearing our costumes and makeup, we would wait quietly through those dark hours before the rising of the Easter sun.

Although this scheme sounded like an adventure to me, it must have seemed sensible to everyone else, including my parents. These were, after all, solid citizens (with the possible exception of Jesus), and everything was well organized by Clarissa, who had assigned each subgroup in the pageant to one of the classrooms surrounding the gym: disciples here, centurions there, holy women in the teachers' lounge. Maggi and I were, however, excluded from her plans because the litter was too fragile to be moved around a lot. Since it would have to stay in the lobby by the trophy case, so would we. (Never a great logician, Clarissa ended up managing a bar on the south side and turning tricks for peanuts.)

At ten thirty on the night of Holy Saturday, I collected my costume from the wardrobe lady and, climbing into it, felt my life tremble on the verge of transformation. Draped in a few folds of light-green semitransparent rayon with a pink leotard underneath, I gave the effect of naked bondage. Around my neck, on each wrist and ankle, a heavy gold band of papier-mâché signed me as slavery's own. Bobbie helped with my makeup: shocking pink voluptuous lips, eyes circled in kohl, dark, dramatic eyebrows where before there had been none to speak of. As the final touch, an orange turban of magnificent implications hid my thin, mousy-brown hair. At last I looked in the mirror. Mine was a face that took makeup well. I was incredibly beautiful. What fabulous photographs would grace the backs of my incredibly passionate novels! To a more discerning eye I resembled nothing so much as a poppy in bloom.

During the dress rehearsal, we all became what we were dressed up to be. The crowd gathered in Jerusalem under the dark, quiet arch of the Field House rafters, so dark the old lost world enclosed us, so quiet the voices of Pontius Pilate and the rest rang out like clanging cymbals. I did not think, This is what it must have been like. Instead, I felt myself a spectator at the run-up to the crucifixion of Jesus, Who was so convincing that I knew I too would believe in Him, were I not such a strange creature, slave to a culture immune to salvation. Despite the glory of His presence, I felt perfectly free to reject Him because . . . well, because I was incredibly beautiful and so enthralled by a life of corruption that I longed for no other. I had seen everything the world had to offer and knew it was mine for the taking. To my slavish mind,

Judas, in a black cape like bat's wings, betrayed nothing at all with his kiss; Herod merely performed a civic duty; and Pontius Pilate—smiling at Mary Magdalene and washing his hands—only did what any man of the world would do.

Rehearsal ended, reality reestablished itself. The bearers gingerly lowered the litter to its spot by the trophy case, and I went with Sonny for cokes and barbecue sandwiches, served up by the Sisters of some Brotherhood. Where was everyone? they wondered, and finally even Sonny left, his mother at the last moment unwilling to let him spend the rest of the night at the Field House. I had another sandwich, then went to look for something. Making a circuit of the dark corridor, I could faintly hear Bill and his crew of fellow firemen inside the gym, hammering away. (Little did we know how many of them would die a few years later in the terrible catastrophe at the cardboard-box factory.) Lights flickered from the classrooms, and I saw that in each lair a party was in full swing. In one Home Ec room, a group of older Jewish matrons placidly chatted over their wine; in another, the half-naked litter bearers, along with a number of centurions, drank beer from dripping bottles pulled from a washtub of ice; and in yet another, the disciples compared Buicks and grass seed and drank surreptitiously from paper cups.

I must have watched these parties for some time because when I returned to the encircling corridor it was no longer empty. Amidst the layered smoke, the ends of cigarettes glowed off and on, off and on. A couple embraced against a clanking locker. Near the shop room, a disciple threw up. Farther along the corridor, another had passed out, and next to the teachers' lounge, the Virgin Mary patted a spear bearer's face with her handkerchief while Herod's guard looked dumbly on, shocked at the sight of blood spilled over a pretty girl. In front of the music room, Mary Magdalene and Pontius Pilate argued with appropriate gestures until she slapped his face. (Later Mrs. Westlake ran off to Chicago with another woman, and Mr. Smith's wife left him for another man.) Near the art room, his head leaning back against the wall, Jesus slept. He came from such good people that seeing all this unaccustomed evil had worn him out. (Eventually he wised up, moved to Denver, and became a popular televangelist until he was caught soliciting a male prostitute.)

My circuit at last brought me back to the front lobby. The litter loomed darkly by the shining trophy case. The curtains parted, and out came Richard, still in Judas's cape. He lit a cigarette, looking for a second exactly like his photograph, then offered a hand to Maggi, inside the litter, and hauled her to her feet. "You're getting fat," he said, and they exchanged some words I couldn't hear before she shuffled off like a housewife doing the morning chores in her bathrobe.

Years later, when I was in college on the East Coast, I went to New York City one weekend with the sole purpose of finding out what had happened to Maggi. I was armed with her address and her current name: Maggi Montefiori. I figured her husband must be a count at least, but he turned out to be an Italian grocer in the East Village. Maggi had cheerfully thickened into an ethnicity that took my breath away. Still only a few years my senior, she was at least twenty years older than I would ever be, and I all but memorized the cans on the shelf, so embarrassed was I to realize that, whatever else she now was, she was at last no longer ordinary. A few years ago I came across her name in the *New York Times*. Alerted by her neighbors, the police had broken into her apartment, where they found her living in great squalor amidst a pride of feral cats.

On that Easter morning, I watched her disappear into the gloom. And then Richard called my name, and I remembered that he was what I had been looking for all along.

"Come here," he said and threw away his cigarette. "At last," he said and, taking my hand, drew me into his embrace.

He kissed me, a hard, sexual kiss. I felt his tongue and a hard rod prodding at my appendix and I was ready to give up everything and follow him when he suddenly drew back and looked at me for a long moment—and then left. His fluttering black cape disguised his disappearance down the long, dark corridor.

I didn't know what to think. I was in such a daze of passion that I simply crawled inside the litter—the feel of his lips on my lips, the feel of his body on mine—and went to sleep. When Maggi woke me up it was almost time for the pageant to begin, and we ran off to hide in a classroom in order to preserve the purity of our illusion for the townspeople who would presently come pouring in.

I hid myself, but what I really wanted to do was burst into the gym, run out onto center court, and shout my good news to the universe. Happiness collected in my chest, in a clump up near my throat, and threatened to swell and swell until it lifted me off my feet and sent me soaring through the roof: Good news! Good news! I wanted to shout. I have been kissed! I am loved! And tears of elation marred what remained of my makeup. What would I have seen had I looked in a mirror? Probably nothing worse than what I saw all around me—for the inspiration of last night's dress rehearsal had disappeared from today's performance. This was the real thing, and oh, what a letdown it was!

First of all, the choir. There it was, all around us, middle-aged women, black and white, dressed in their new Easter outfits, belting out a medley of favorite hymns. How amazed the townspeople of Jerusalem would have been by such an occurrence, not to mention the thumping piano! And then, the light. Either we'd gotten a late start or sunrise was early that year, because instead of performing under the stage lights that turned every sequin to a precious jewel, we acted out our fable in broad daylight that revealed every lie for what it was. The audience visibly glared down in disappointment, while, heads throbbing, mouths full of ashes, we welcomed the Reverend Johnny into Jerusalem and Maggi was converted to a myth. The hungover Kiwanis Club had a tough time in the Garden—so many of them, alas! destined to go bankrupt over the next twenty years! Richard kissed Johnny in betrayal. And Mr. Smith, the banker, did his bit for justice, while, delivered right on time by his mother, Sonny out-Heroded Herod in a pink wig and false eyelashes. Reverend Johnny floated down the aisle toting his cardboard cross; Bobbie—wearing a padded jock strap and real leather gauntlets—gambled for the robe; and Mrs. Westlake and Donna (with Clarissa in attendance) dropped by a wobbling tomb to discover Johnny risen from the dead.

And yet I looked on this performance with eyes of mercy, for I had eaten of the fruit, and it had brought me the knowledge of good and evil. I saw that if we resembled the characters we portrayed, it was because we were all ordinary people who shared a sexual wisdom of which this pageant was only a pale metaphor. Good news, indeed! I had been kissed! Really kissed! I had that to hold on to! I could hardly wait for this travesty to end so that I could go out and announce to the whole world the wonderful thing that had happened to me.

Well, that had almost happened to me. For, as the pageant drew to a close and I changed out of my costume and went off to meet my parents in the parking lot, I began to wonder if anything at all had actually happened. After all, he had only kissed me! Maybe I had merely experienced a nonevent surrounded by a lot of beautiful notions that were, in the end, meaningful only for other people? Had I really embraced the mystery? Maybe I had better hold my tongue until I understood why I alone was destined to be unique.

*

And unique in one sense I clearly am. Almost unique. I have been told that, by current estimates, eighty-five percent of American women are molested when they are children, nineteen percent by a close relative. If these figures are correct, then I am at least atypical—for I belong to the unmolested fifteen percent. I suppose a critic could say that Richard did not need to molest me physically, having already seduced me to a fare-thee-well, and it is true that for many years I never thought of Richard's kiss with anything but elation. I would like to tell you that his one kiss encompassed everything I needed to know of love, and its memory rendered me immune from temptation for years and years. I would like to tell you that I am writing this story during my retirement, after a long career as the head librarian of a private Episcopalian girls' school out in the Virginia countryside. I would like to tell you this, but of course it would not be true, even in a fictional sense. I can, however, tell you that I eventually emerged from Muncie as clean as if it had never existed, as if the Lynds had come back in 1960 and dropped a neutron bomb on all its typicality.

And I can also tell you truthfully that I continue to feel a certain elation over the kiss. From time to time I have even felt free to regret that Richard didn't take me into the litter and really make me his own. Even if he was only a child molester, I loved him, and I would gladly have been his, and of course I am free to feel this regret because he was a child molester who looked at me and at the critical moment—stopped. Why? Did he look at me and see innocence? I was no more innocent than Maggi had been. Or did he suddenly realize on Easter morning that what he liked to do was wrong? No, I am told that child molesters never learn. Did he look at me and see futility? that I would grow up one day, as Maggi had done? No, child molesters do not expect eternal love and always look forward to the next avatar. So what did he see in me that made him stop?

I believe that as he leaned over to kiss me, he saw his reflection in the pupils of my wide-open eyes. And in that reflected Judas he saw

45

a symbol of the child who would betray him! Just when he'd almost gotten his degree! Just when he had a good teaching job lined up for next year! There was no way he could look into my eyes and see that, a Judas long after the fact, I would wait sixty years to tell this story.

Which I have now done. Is mine the corrupted voice of a victim accepting blame? Am I a pale negative of those women who cry in front of congressional committees and accuse on television talk shows? In either case, Richard needn't have worried. Fantasy or trauma, ordinary or strange, shaggy dog or purebred pooch, my story only testifies to an absence of effect, not unlike the results of our reenacted fertility rite that Easter morning. We performed our totally inadequate rite, and yet there was no corn blight that year. No drought did in the soybeans. There wasn't even a strike by the UAW. Of course it's true that during the next thirty years Delco Battery and Warner Gear and all those little machine shops that, taken together, had ultimately been able to build a car, all of those left Muncie so that nothing of any industrial importance is produced there anymore. You can imagine what the index of *The Golden Bough* would make of it:

• Child molester at half-assed Easter Pageant; see General Motors, the end of.

Still, it remains a fact that as far as homeopathic magic is concerned, our little Easter pageant had absolutely no effect, one way or another. And so it was with Richard's kiss. It did nothing to me one way or another, and when you get right down to it, my only real regret is that in spite of all that early exposure I detest the theater and, except for No and Kabuki, in which no faith in reality is expected, am apt to sit through whatever I am forced to watch with my hands twisting and my teeth clenched in a boredom that is indistinguishable from anxiety. Comedy, tragedy, it's all the same to me.

Sins against Animals

In 1965, a few months before graduation, a man from the Job Corps penetrated to the upper floors of Main, the building at Vassar College where the seniors lived, a presumably impregnable niche. There he found corridors lined with astonished women who were more than willing to go teach remedial English, math, and social studies to high school dropouts: tender, long-legged birds bred to serve, stuffed with good intentions and an amazing amount of useless knowledge, eager to fly the coop.

"Lambs to the slaughter," Diana teased her friend Eleanor. Diana was engaged to a student at Yale Law School and had been accepted as a graduate student in Art History. Her future was assured, but for a moment she felt inadequate, even wrong, because Eleanor, who had no plans at all, had graciously accepted the kind invitation of the man from the Job Corps.

In Diana's eyes, it was all too typical that Eleanor would fall for this offer. She was forever going off on blind dates with boys who managed to break her heart within six hours, or crying her eyes out over somebody's brother at Hamilton who hadn't asked her out for a second date, or mooning around for months over some jerk from home who had never asked her out in the first place. Still, the Job Corps was clearly a worthy cause, a chance to do some real good in the world, and so for a day or two Diana felt guilty that she was too cynical to give it a try.

For a year and a half, Eleanor taught reading and grammar to boys from the ghetto who were getting a second chance—or sometimes a third or a fourth. Eleanor's family—prosperous Quakers and liberal Democrats who had named their eldest daughter after their heroine—

approved of her job; the boys were by and large appreciative; and at first every small gain counted for a lot. Many of her Vassar friends who were working for the Job Corps seemed to fall in love with the other instructors; they were all the age for marriage. Eleanor fell in love with nobody and, faced with melioration on a day-to-day basis, rapidly grew disenchanted. At the end of the second year, she left the Job Corps to join a project in New York called Neighborhoods Inc.

Neighborhoods (cynics joked about capitalizing the second "h") was an offshoot of a drug-treatment program called Resurrection, which—flush with hopeful funding—used the relatively new technique of group dynamics to break down the old personality of the drug addict and replace it with a new, nonaddictive self. Although the group therapy was admittedly brutal, the reconstruction was complete, and—in theory—once the addict lost his old destructive defenses in Resurrection, he was free to use his new self to help others in Neighborhoods. And he would do so with the zeal of the converted, which burns with abandoned shame. In practice, Neighborhoods sent the ex-addict out with a conventional social worker to live on a deteriorating street in Harlem. Together, they would gradually rehabilitate the block. They would begin with their own building, for example, by organizing an entryway cleanup. Then they would bully the relevant city agency into picking up the trash or find pro bono lawyers to sue the landlord. Next, gradually, they would urge people to form tenant associations to do more complex things like neighborhood patrols against drug trafficking. Along the way, the ex-addict would gain confidence and self-esteem and recruit other addicts into the Resurrection treatment program.

The success of this venture depended heavily on the quality of the social workers, and these were in short supply, perhaps because Neighborhoods demanded that they undergo the same group therapy as the addicts. Soon Neighborhoods had to abandon the requirement of conventional degrees.

Not with alarm, however, because what they really needed were not social workers but responsible, well-educated, middle-class individuals—like Eleanor, who had, nevertheless, majored in sociology in college.

No one worried about what the self of a reconstructed social worker would amount to. For example, would it continue to be responsible, well educated, and middle class? Certainly if Eleanor ever considered this issue, she forgot it in the press of learning how to organize neighborhoods. For three months, she studied in the main Resurrection-Neighborhoods office in the East Sixties, and then she had her group therapy session. Five quasi-social workers and ten ex-addicts locked themselves in a room for seventy-two hours. No one was allowed to sleep; food was delivered through a crack in the door; the room filled with smoke as each social-worker type was criticized in turn. Nothing was off limits. In Eleanor's case, everyone focused on her middle-class background and education, although a few raised their voices against her dowdy clothes, her gently whining voice, and what one ex-addict called her "bourgeois sentimental romantic attitude about fucking."

Eleanor had always accepted guilt readily, readily deferring to others, especially men. This attitude aided in her speedy self-destruction by the group. Her old personality was obliterated in tears of self-hatred, and after twelve hours of sleep she awoke feeling reborn and thoroughly capable of reforming the —th block of —st Street.

With two ex-addicts, Fred and Goose, Eleanor moved into a run-down building, where, in spite of the 1968 riots, they enjoyed a productive season. Both the entryway and the alley were cleaned up; a bake sale earned more than a hundred dollars; an Anti-rat Day was projected for the fall. And in July Eleanor fell in love with the star of the whole program, Addison, an ex-addict who'd worked his way up the ladder to become one of the directors of Resurrection itself.

Fred and Goose moved into the building next door, and Addison moved in with Eleanor, who walked around all day on the cusp of significance. Her life had achieved its form, and no matter what happened to her in the future, she knew she would always remember this summer: Her work was important; this was true love! For the first and last time in her life, she reported her doings to the *Vassar Alumnae Magazine.*

*

Meanwhile, Diana finished her course work, passed her orals, started her dissertation, and made wedding plans. The two women seldom saw each other, but they occasionally talked on the phone and once in a great while exchanged letters. Even in sporadic context, they were important to each other. They came from the same small industrial city, a grimy ash heap dumped on the green Ohio countryside. Diana's family was Republican and Presbyterian instead of Democratic and Quaker, significant cause for all sorts of divergences of taste and opinion. Diana, the two women agreed, was in thrall by birth to a sterner vision of humanity; Eleanor, they likewise agreed, was free to improve the human lot. With so much symbolism at hand, they needed very little of each other's actual presence to feel themselves friends for life. Diana loved Eleanor's easily dejected idealism; Eleanor admired Diana's free-ranging skepticism. Diana felt a little more solid and real having Eleanor as a friend, while Eleanor felt a little more savvy and energetic knowing that Diana admired her. Neither felt substantially more self-confident and less to blame, but—as they frequently pointed out to each other—there was nothing in either of their backgrounds that encouraged those feelings.

And so it was not surprising that when the drug dealers murdered Addison in the entryway of the apartment building, Eleanor called Diana to come help her with his funeral.

Diana was so reluctant that it took her almost twenty-four hours to get herself onto the midmorning train to New York. The bright sunlight on the dirty windows seemed to point a finger at the misfit who rode the rails outside the dawn-and-dusk structure of commuting. The air had the superfluous metallic aftertaste of vitamin pills with iron. It was early May, yet hot as midsummer, and the dirty plush upholstery of the seats reminded Diana that the last time she'd visited Eleanor she'd broken out in a rash.

During that visit, six months before, Diana had, at first, found Eleanor much the same as ever: a C+ student whose highest goal was to be a wife and mother; a nonjudgmental sort who still believed in good manners as the outward sign of virtue. Her slum apartment featured cloth napkins and a guest bedroom. Soon, however, Diana found herself wondering if Eleanor hadn't really changed, for as she spoke of her work on the block, of the people she'd met, of the injustice of their lives, she ignored Addison's antics, which in earlier times would have immediately reduced her to tears.

Eleanor hardly seemed to notice the glass Addison threw at her early in the evening, nor did she seem particularly upset when he called her a rich white bitch and then stormed out to spend the night with an old girlfriend. Eleanor seemed not to notice his absence; she continued to talk about the embryonic tenants' association. Diana eventually concluded that radical political conviction had overtaken Eleanor's former emotional liberalism. The women sat there all night, smoking, drinking, Eleanor calmly going into some detail about the dynamics of the entry cleanup, Diana scratching and waiting nervously for Addison's return. She could only wonder at the political wisdom that promoted indifference to such manipulation, an invulnerable wisdom that made her feel utterly inadequate.

Now, on the train, Diana itched in anticipation, as if the dirty plush and the dusty glass were vehicles through which the spirit of history conveyed to a worn-out civilization the gospel of a revolution to come.

*

After the murder, Eleanor decided to stay with some friends on the Upper West Side. Mrs. Berke edited a glossy women's magazine, while Mr. Berke was legal counsel to an enormous labor union. Their living room was full of objects signifying culture, wealth, and beauty without in the least suggesting the traditional or the exclusive. Diana knew this was no mean feat, and Eleanor sat in the midst of it all, pale, calm, unusually confident. The Berkes were nowhere in sight. Addison hung in the air like the smile of the Cheshire Cat.

Eleanor explained what had happened: She had been lying in bed reading, waiting for Addison, who'd been out at some meeting, she wasn't sure where. About three in the morning she thought she heard him come in. Since their apartment was on the second floor at the front corner of the building, she could hear things in the entryway—but only if she already more or less knew what she was listening to. She thought she'd heard him come in—didn't she hear her name?—but he didn't come up, and so, at first, she assumed she'd been mistaken. Then, after ten minutes or so, she decided that the sound she'd heard had most certainly been "Eleanor." And so she put on her robe and slippers and went down—even though she knew this was not a safe thing to do. The entryway was clean now, but it was still Harlem and three in the morning.

She found Addison dead. In his arm, a hypodermic needle bobbled up and down like the stinger of a gigantic mosquito. She pulled out the needle and tried to revive him. Apparently the murderer had waited in the shadowy entryway and stabbed Addison with the needle as he walked in the door. Unused as Addison now was to the drug, he had died almost immediately of an overdose with just time enough to shout out her name—and now she wasn't even sure about that.

Diana couldn't believe it. "It seems so risky. Don't you have to hit a vein or something?"

"Oh, it happens all the time," Eleanor assured her. "It's the way drug dealers handle people who interfere with business. Addison's death shows we're having some effect. He's a real hero."

Diana resigned herself to this interpretation. "What can I do to help?"

The funeral, it seemed, was already arranged. Addison had been raised by a great-aunt who had firm ideas to which Eleanor—given the aunt's age, poverty, and race—felt bound to accede. Only innumerable details remained. Could Diana go back to the apartment and pack? Eleanor had no desire to live there anymore. If Diana could get everything ready tonight, then tomorrow, after the memorial service, the Mass, the burial, and the Resurrection/Neighborhoods party, Eleanor would move into a different apartment on a new block where—all that work gone to waste!—she could start over.

*

Two hours later, a taxi driver helped Diana carry some empty boxes to the entryway of Eleanor's apartment building. Outside, the streets of Harlem looked untouched by Neighborhoods. The entryway, however, showed signs of improvement. The twelve mailboxes were still broken, a dangling bare bulb still tenuously provided light, the elevator was still boarded against use—but the tile floor was clean and the walls recently painted. The scene of the crime, and yet it looked no different for that. Was this because places are impervious to the events that take place in them or because murder is so common that its mark is indistinguishable to the eye? The art historian in Diana considered edifices temporal and sacred, modern and ancient, vernacular and monumental, ugly and beautiful: Was any without its crime? Although no drug dealer had reason to murder her, she felt a certain relief when she had locked herself safely in Eleanor's apartment. The door had two deadbolts and a chain.

As she remembered from her other visit, Eleanor had taken pains to set a good example: lots of paint, new linoleum, curtains—yet it wouldn't take all that long to dismantle. Brick-and-board bookcases full of Eleanor's college paperbacks, the minimum number of dishes, a few old dresses in the closet. Eleanor's clothes could go into her suitcases; Addison's things, into a box for the aunt, who could also have the furniture, such as it was. Wouldn't it just be easier to open the door and commit the contents to the neighborhood? This wasn't her decision, however, so she started to pack.

Diana had actually cleared one closet before she noticed the cat. Orange and white, pink nose, calm yellow eyes, a young altered male: the quintessential Ohio cat. Back home, he would sleep in the window box among the geraniums. Here, he sat on top of the icebox, patiently waiting for cockroaches? rats? Investigation revealed a litter box in the shower (of all places!) and a box of Friskies. The cat ate with some eagerness and offered a purr to Diana's caressing hand. After eating, he took up a new position on top of the bookcase.

A call to Eleanor reached Mrs. Berke, who said that the sedative had taken effect and Eleanor was out cold for the night. She had mentioned something about getting rid of the cat. Mrs. Berke suggested the Animal Shelter.

Well, not tonight, thought Diana. She would call him Joe until Eleanor told her his real name. The Animal Shelter. Wasn't that the same as the Pound?

The apartment was hot and airless, so Diana opened the window onto the fire escape. The window lacked a screen, and as she packed she began to hope that Joe would take this occasion to claim his freedom and his life. The Animal Shelter, indeed! But Joe hunkered down into the shape of a casserole, paws neatly folded in front of him, totally uninterested in escaping into Harlem: I am your responsibility, he seemed to say. She quickly grew used to his presence and, around eight, rather than venture out onto the streets, shared a can of tuna fish with him. By midnight, when she was down to the odds and ends, she was sorry to see Joe accept self-determination and disappear through the window and down the fire escape, leaving her alone.

Alone. She thought about where she was and shut and locked the window. If Addison saw Eleanor as a rich white bitch, how would his neighbors see her? Would they be predisposed to mercy on individual grounds? What grounds could these possibly be? Perhaps she had sweated so much that her electrolytes were out of order, for suddenly she was sick with fear. She draped towels over the front windows to protect herself from prying eyes, checked the locks, and had almost decided that she was safe when her anxieties suddenly veered in Joe's direction.

He was out there on the streets, alone. Wouldn't he be lost? Freedom was all very well, but who would feed him and take him to the vet when he got sick? This is not reasonable, Diana told herself, but she couldn't keep herself from wondering if life were worth living for Joe on the streets. Who would love him? Where would he sleep at night? Prey to what dogs and ruthless children, large rats, faceless violence, random cars? How would he feel if he climbed back up the fire escape and found the window locked against him? She unlocked the window and raised it a cat-sized crack.

It was late. Leaving her clothes on, she turned out the light and lay down on the bare mattress, face to the fire escape. Anyone could climb up that fire escape, crawl in that window, murder her. Stomach churning with apprehension, afraid to open her eyes, Diana lay in the darkness until she couldn't bear it any longer. She jumped up and closed the window.

Then all she could imagine was Joe, his calm yellow eyes staring hopelessly in through the window, abandoned. ... It was at least three in the morning. She must try to be sensible. She must get control of herself. She got up and opened the window. When her mother had had Diana's cat Snowball put to sleep—at the vet's, surely; not the Pound—she had told Diana that Snowball had gone to live in the country. Remembering this, Diana again felt betrayed and sick with helplessness and rage. She thought of the black man who would climb the fire escape, slip through the window, and stand above her bed, looking down on her in a long, meditative moment of revenge and uttering a prayer to the hungry god before he strangled her and dragged her twitching body to the bathtub where he set to work dismembering her and throwing gobbets of her body all over Harlem, like that argument—or was it a poem?—about the ceiling of the Sistine Chapel: Divided up so that everyone could have an equal share, it amounted to less than a grain of salt. No matter how much they hated her, no matter how wrong she was, there wasn't enough to go around. No loaves and fishes, she, and so doomed to be inadequate.

When she woke up just before dawn, she found Joe in her arms like a teddy bear, his head on her shoulder, purring away with all the satisfaction of the prodigal returned. His fur was cold and slightly damp. After an adventure he'd come home to stay. Diana fell back to sleep without a care in the world. She did not bother to get up and close the window, for who in the world would climb through a window to get her?

In the morning, she gave Joe the last can of tuna, cleaned out the icebox, assembled the garbage, and watched the rooms—stripped of their trappings—rejoin themselves to the slum that shimmered outside the windows. Joe ate his tuna fish, used his pan, and took a prolonged and thorough bath, biting into the spaces between his clear pink toe-pads, chewing down a rough claw, and finally sharpening the whole set on the black-and-white-striped, brown-puddled mattress. Shortly thereafter, Eleanor arrived with Mr. Berke, who loaded up his station wagon with Eleanor's belongings and drove off, leaving the women to deal with Joe, whose name turned out to be Brahms.

Brahms was a problem because he was Addison's cat. He slept on Addison's side of the bed. Addison had loved him. Eleanor had never taken to Brahms, nor he to her. Like Diana, she was not intrinsically fond of cats, so Siamese elegance or tuxedo wit was necessary to seize her fancy. Eleanor had asked Addison's great-aunt to take Brahms, but she had refused, hinting at darker responsibilities. "You don't want him, do you?" Eleanor asked with a thoughtlessness that almost made Diana lose her temper.

"I'm going to Italy for a year! He's not *my* boyfriend's cat! Isn't there anybody at Resurrection who can take him? What about one of your *neighbors*? Look! why don't you send him home to Ohio? Your mother can always find room for a cat." Snowball had gone to live in the country; why not a real version of an old lie?

"He would always remind me of Addison."

"You really don't think you're going to forget him, do you?" Diana saw, nevertheless, that this was no time to press a point, and so the women took a taxi to the Animal Shelter, which looked unavoidably like a gigantic oven from which Joe/Brahms had but a seventy-two-hour reprieve. Handing him over, Diana couldn't bring herself to meet his eyes; even so, she could feel his purr. A good animal, he made himself easy to dispose of, unlike Addison, who would require the next six hours to make his adieux.

Diana gave in: Okay, okay, I'll come back. Even though I don't really like cats. You can stay in Ohio with *my* mother until I get back from Italy. Then you can live with me.

Finally she could look into his calm yellow eyes and prepare herself for the next ordeal.

*

At eleven, there was an open-casket viewing at the funeral home in the Bronx—round one for the grieving aunt, a wizened sorceress complete with turban and mumbling false teeth. She was accompanied by two small brown boys in little black suits and white shirts whose overpowering resemblance to Addison spelled trouble. Diana dismissed them with "different mores," but she could tell that Eleanor was hurt as well as surprised.

A record player, hidden somewhere underneath the casket, played Vivaldi's The Four Seasons over and over and over again as Addison contemplated eternity with smug pleasure, like the cat—Diana unavoidably thought—who had swallowed the canary. For a solid hour the bigwigs of Resurrection praised Addison to the skies. Under Diana's gaze, his expression turned to one of polite disbelief: This was me? You've got to be kidding! Eleanor sat in the front row by the aunt and the little boys, who laughed, squirmed, hit each other, and looked more like Addison by the minute.

At one o'clock, round two for the aunt, an hour-long Mass echoed through a Catholic church half a block from the funeral home. The church dwarfed both coffin and mourners, who had already shrunk in number, about half going off in search of lunch. Had Addison been christened and confirmed here? Certainly none of the mourners were Catholics—not even the aunt, it would seem, for she neither rose nor kneeled nor took Communion but sat solidly at Eleanor's side, while the little boys took a well-deserved nap. Diana herself struggled to stay awake. The priest called Addison Edison.

At two thirty they left the church for the cemetery, which was far away on Long Island—round three for the aunt.

Eleanor climbed into a silver-gray limousine directly behind the hearse. Since she was then joined by the aunt and the boys, Diana abruptly ducked into the next limo, and so near was her escape that it took a few moments before she could calm down and focus on the other passengers, five more-or-less reformed addicts, one of whom had the shakes. By the time she took them in—braids, elf locks, turbans, beads, dashikis, bells, caftans, and eyes incapable of meeting hers—the cortege was off and they were stuck with each other.

No one uttered a sound, and Diana was struck with the wild impulse to apologize for her shoes. These were plain white pumps with two-inch heels—and Memorial Day was a full three weeks away! They were the only shoes she had that went with the only dress she owned that was long enough to wear to a funeral; everything else was mini. Still, she knew they were wrong; her feet looked enormous, and their whiteness kept catching her eye, and she also wanted to apologize for drinking spirits before dinner unmixed with wine or juice, for wearing nylon underwear, for eating egg salad in restaurants, for loving a man with a mustache, for smoking in public, for chewing gum even in private, for never really loving anyone or anything, for doing all these things her mother had told her never to do, but even though she wished to apologize, she had actually done none of these things, except wear white shoes and fail to love, and so, instead of apologizing, she fell asleep.

As she slept she heard the men talk about what a hero Addison was. She heard because of the translating power of the unconscious, for when she woke up, she couldn't understand a word they were saying; it was English, but not to her ear. Accustomed to her presence, they talked on among themselves while she stared out the window at a cemetery so big it threatened to swallow up everyone in the world.

Traffic was heavy. Their cortege passed four funerals, clusters of cars waiting at the side of the road. Two other funerals passed in the opposite direction, going home for the night, funerals no longer. A dark-green military truck whizzed past and pulled off to the side of the road. A group of soldiers jumped out, guns at the ready, and ran off toward a hidden ceremony, the bugle player trotting along behind.

Ten minutes later, their cortege pulled over to the side of the road. At the grave, a short walk away, Eleanor stood with Addison's aunt and the little boys, who stood still for once, quiet, in a daze. The ex-addicts and social-worker types arranged themselves in twos and threes. Struck by the sight of the open grave, no one talked.

Diana stood alone on the edge of the mourners and watched the green truck drive up. The troops jumped out and charged up to the grave, late as usual, behind in their work, the bugler still lagging in the rear, a fat boy about twenty. The soldiers were all young, with smooth, blank faces that suggested boredom. Were they thinking of the battles they were missing and the heroes who were falling in them? They did not look at the bizarre crowd that faced them across the grave: voodoo spirits, the ghosts of ancient tribesmen. Their eyes stuck to the middle distance as the priest rushed through his lines, calling down mercy on Addison, whom he continued to call Edison. The soldiers fired their salute, listened to the final "Taps"—how many times today?—and then ran back to the truck. If they only hurried, might they not catch up with that elusive war halfway around the world?

Eleanor threw a single red rose into the grave, and Diana leaped forward to claim her firmly by the elbow. She steered her back to the gray limo, told the driver to make it snappy, and left the aunt and children to the priest. Never had she been so hungry in her life.

*

At first the women sat in apprehensive silence as the chauffeur tried to make his way through the worst of rush hour with something passing for speed. At last, Diana told him to slow down or to feel all right about going so slowly, for they were in fact going almost nowhere, only sitting in the middle of six lanes of cars surrounded by acres of houses that looked like more cars.

When Eleanor said, in a perfectly serious tone, "Wasn't that beautiful?" Diana raised the window that cut them off from the driver and waited in silence until Eleanor came to her senses. "Actually, I suppose it was pretty ridiculous." As yellow as the flowers in her dress, Eleanor no longer looked like her old self.

"Well, it's hard to stage a funeral that pleases everyone. You did a great job, given the aunt and all. We're probably the only ones who think it was ridiculous. Everybody else probably thinks it was the perfect funeral for a hero. But really, Eleanor—"

"Weren't the soldiers a stitch?"

"Does the cemetery just throw them in free?"

"Oh, no. They're the real thing. Addison's aunt wants to get benefits for the children. I guess she thought a military funeral would establish her claims. He might have been in the army, but I'm sure he never actually fought in anything. And he wasn't a Catholic either. And the little boys don't even have the same mother. I didn't know about them. About the children. I knew about the other women."

"Maybe she's counting on help from the Church?"

"The whole thing was a fraud." Eleanor began to cry again.

In disgust the chauffeur turned off the highway. Around them endlessly stretched something that was not Manhattan. "Now, now. Symbols are everything. Maybe it's best to think of the whole thing as a sign of good intentions. Addison probably believed in something, and if he didn't, he probably wished he did." Twaddle, Diana thought, a language I speak fluently. "And as for his not being a real soldier, he's a real hero. You should have heard the men in my car."

"I can't go to this party."

"Thank God; let's not. Why don't—"

"He wasn't murdered. He killed himself. Maybe by accident. Maybe not. We had a fight. I told him I was tired of his stunts, tired of him. I wanted him to move out. I told him I'd only put up with him for so long because he loved me more than I loved him and I've never had that happen before. He started crying. He said he was a failure at everything. He said he might just as well go back on drugs. I told him I was tired of his threats. He stormed out, and I went to bed. I was so relieved to get rid of him and his . . . his stupidity that I felt I could sleep forever. My whole life, all I've wanted was to be loved, and he even made me tired of that."

"How did he die?"

"The rest of what I said was more or less true. I heard him in the entryway. He woke me up shouting my name. I think. Eleanor, or Dirty Whore. Who knows? Anyway, when I got downstairs he was dead. He'd taken an overdose, I don't think on purpose. I think it was just to say, see what you made me do. I don't know. I pulled out the needle and tried to get as many of my fingerprints on it as possible."

"Stop the car!" Diana demanded. They were probably somewhere in Brooklyn, not that it mattered. They were trapped somewhere in an endless city, and this corner was as good as any. In fact, after they got out, they discovered both a Chinese restaurant and a movie theater.

They decided to see the movie first to calm down. Science fiction. Diana had trouble getting into it: Charlton Heston crashes his space ship onto a planet that turns out to be run by apes; not a thoroughly bad lot, they view the subjected human species with a mixture of pity and disgust. About the time Diana understood that this was New York City after the nuclear holocaust, she also noticed that the apes bore a strong facial resemblance to the ex-addicts in the limo. It was Eleanor, however, who actually said, "Is this movie as racist as I think it is?"

"I don't know," answered Diana, "but it's certainly anti-simian. Perhaps we should leave?"

Next door, at the Chinese restaurant, the menu was elaborate, and the women tried all sorts of strange things, for in the long run, what did they have to lose? After two bottles of a wine that tasted of mothballs, Eleanor told Diana that Addison had been wonderful in bed; he'd made her feel that she was the most exciting person in the world. Maybe she had loved him. Maybe he had been murdered—no, she didn't love him. He was just a manipulator—always trying to protect a self he didn't have. He bored her. He betrayed her. All the time. How did he have the nerve to bore her *and* betray her? She didn't love him, and, exciting or not, she'd gotten tired of having him love her.

Diana felt relieved. No matter who loved whom, it was just love after all. Not politics, not a new self, just bourgeois sentimental romantic love. If group dynamics had eradicated Eleanor's personality, Nature had issued a near-perfect duplicate. Diana felt so much better about her friend that she didn't allow herself the additional luxury of self-disgust. So she had never loved anyone. So what? Instead, she suggested that they borrow Mr. Berke's station wagon and drive home.

Eleanor agreed, and before dawn the next morning, they set out, Diana so elated that she drove all the way back to Ohio, where the city didn't go on forever but stopped at the edge of the country so that you had to drive out through fields of soybeans and corn and hogs just to get to the country club. Back to Ohio, where Addison's ghost could be laid to rest in no time.

*

Eighteen years later, Eleanor is the head of a progressive school in Chicago. She has had many lovers but none whom she felt like marrying, although last year she adopted an orphan from El Salvador and is now thinking that the divorced head of a local boys' school might do as a stepfather. He is wild about her, passion's eternal response to indifference. Eleanor has fallen into a bad habit.

She thinks about Addison from time to time and wonders what would have happened if she'd managed to love him more than he loved her. Would she have gone on loving all her life? But she hadn't. And what if he had been murdered? Would she have been frightened enough to marry a dull accountant as soon as possible after his death? Would she have had three children just to be safe? Would she still lie awake at night feeling relieved that Addison died—and feeling guilty that she feels relieved?

Diana is divorced and no longer close to Eleanor—time and distance have intervened—and she never thinks of Addison if she remembers him at all. And yet—as she is fond of telling her students—there is a God in Heaven, and He is a just God, and so Diana has terrible nightmares every year in late spring, a time of year that is very hard for animals. It is worse than early spring, when nameless eggs splash, unidentifiable, on the sidewalk. The young are just as vulnerable in the late spring, but by then everybody has gotten to know one another.

A little starling trembles on the edge of his nest and breaks his neck when he hits the concrete. His brother lands back down, beak upward. The old Siamese cat remembers better days and eats them both while entertaining the fantasy that he has actually hunted them down. He enjoyed watching the nest from the bedroom window, and all day he feels vaguely dissatisfied: Something is coming. What is it?

Paths cross in troubling ways. A mother duck leads her brood across a major thoroughfare in rush hour, heading toward the nearest body of water. She is hit by a taxi but loses only one duckling and a wing. Mother squirrels dash across the traffic, on their way to their babies in the trees. One is hit in the hindquarters but drags herself across the rest of the street and disappears into the bushes. Is it for the best if she makes it back to the nest? A raccoon lies twitching in the road until a carful of teenagers swerves to hit the body. Blood spurts, parts scatter, crows gather, raccoon flattens. Soon there is only a hairy pelt; then, only a grease spot.

Diana dreams the cat dream and wakes up screaming from something she can't remember. A grin forgives her, fades away into the hanging fern at the window, not a cat at all. The lights in the bedrooms of the neighboring apartment houses accuse her of betrayal and breach of trust. She lies there in bed, exhausted and weeping, sweating, shaking, trying her best to remember what it is she has forgotten to do.

The Ring and the Box It Came In

It was the night of Open Studios at the American Academy in Rome, the night when the fellows show their projects and various friends of the Academy as well as the trustees come to look . . . and of course silently to judge.

Just to be at the Academy is a great honor. To have the Rome Prize on your résumé announces a high level of achievement. Even the Academy's location on a hill in Trastevere and its far-reaching views suggest the benefits of intellectual and artistic superiority. The fellows are divided into two fields of study, organized, according to Academy literature, less by subject matter than by differences of methodology: the School of Classical Studies and the School of Fine Arts. This story springs from the second, a more literal field in this instance because Jack was a young landscape architect from Indiana. To him, a high elevation, a wide prospect, even a field of study, figured all the more potently as metaphors because he was unusually aware of their literal vehicles.

In his application to the Academy, Jack had submitted a project exploring physical landscape changes in the war-torn country of Iraq. From the beginning, he knew he had a winner. The war was so unpopular with American intellectuals that a design project proclaiming its wrongness would have immediate appeal—especially since he did not intend to limit his work to an investigation of cultural conditions: abandoned houses in Sunni/Shiite neighborhoods, for example, or uncovered Saddam execution sites. Instead, his study would explain how the landscape proclaims war and peace on its own terms, in the physical destruction of battlegrounds and their subsequent regeneration by various weeds and grasses. He called his project "Volunteers in Hell."

Although candidates propose a project in their application, it is not unusual for some more enticing topic to beckon to them during their stay in Rome. After Jack arrived at the Academy, a month of consideration more or less exhausted the Iraqi landscape, and he shifted his focus, if only to have something to talk about at meals. He now investigated weeds in the Roman landscape by means of amusing photographs that showed everything from weeds on the Roman aqueduct in the Baldassarre Peruzzi murals at the Villa Farnesina to the ubiquitous weediness of Piranesi to the very real weeds in the drainpipes of the Vatican. Look out a window anywhere in Rome and there was a weed, evidence of what satisfied the Italian taste in landscape as well as a profound recognition of the human condition and a cynical long view of the fate of empires. Jack was not pleased with this project, however, because in execution it so closely resembled the chief activity of the tourist hordes: taking photographs. Yet he could think of nothing else to do. The approach of intellectual landscape architecture—planting an orderly bed of weeds, for example, or planting vegetables in cardboard boxes—seemed too clichéd, and writing an article, too aloof. Besides, he couldn't believe that the article hadn't already been written.

It might be said that Jack's difficulty in transforming his topics into definite form stemmed from the deception that clouded his real motive for applying to the Academy. He was using the Rome Prize not to pursue an academic study or create a work of art but for another, more prosaic purpose: career change. If Jack had run this past others, he would probably have learned that it was a time-honored custom at the Academy. But he hadn't, and so he felt just a little bit bogus. In his case, he was using the Rome Prize to effect a graceful segue out of his partnership in an unsuccessful three-person landscape firm specializing in Indianapolis residential work to a more reliable academic position at a large Midwestern university. Nevertheless, he really was grateful to have some free time because he would eventually need articles, a book even, to get tenure in the department. In fact, his old professor of landscape architecture had suggested a wonderful topic, a look at landscape architecture graduate students over the past forty years, an updating of the Fine Report. Jack thought a great deal about this study. It would have a real impact on the field and, beautifully illustrated with student projects, could be used for fund-raising. Unfortunately, it had nothing to do with Rome.

Happily, Jack talked with Professor Caldwell several times a month, and he had proposed another, more Roman, topic, one that Jack had subsequently pursued to realization and now, on the night of Open Studios, exhibited for the judgment of others.

The wine was out, some crackers and cheese displayed on a table, and as he waited, Jack gradually took notice of the numerous visitors who made their way to his studio, took a quick look, and left, only to congregate—that is, eat and drink, look and talk—in other studios, especially Gus Franklin's, which was right next door to Jack's.

Gus had chosen an ordinary project to justify his year in Rome, a study of modern art museums. This had resulted in dozens of photographs of existing museums as well as models of two others that Gus himself would like to design, one in an old parking garage, another in an abandoned big-box store. What this project would probably result in, Jack thought, was more actual work for Gus's already established firm. He was pleased that he himself had been more risk-taking, more politically aggressive. His own project would result in no built work, but it was intellectually admirable as well as educational, especially when he thought of it as a special exhibit sponsored by the School of Architecture during his second or third year at the university. It wasn't an article, but it showed that his heart was in the right place and his eye was keen, things that would undoubtedly count a great deal with some future tenure committee. In fact, Jack was proud of his concept—half visual, half written; half Rome, half Indiana; half architecture, half landscape—and he was confident that its edgy nature was responsible for the fact—yes, sad fact—that it was not attracting much attention.

An hour into Open Studios and only his wife and a few of her friends lingered in the room, and as the minutes wore on and the social rumble reverberated through the halls of the Academy and specifically in Gus's studio next door, Jack interpreted this lack of appreciation as artistic justification. If something was so ignored, it just proved how much it was needed.

Ned, a modern dancer, came in, poured a glass of wine, and joined the group over in the corner talking with Linda, Jack's wife. Jack decided to join them. He didn't talk but stood facing the wall of photographs, watching people wander in, take a look, leave.

One wall was covered with black-and-white photographs: crowd scenes, fairly close-up shots showing the top half of a sea of angry young men conservatively coiffed and clad in suits and ties. To the knowledgeable—those who bothered to read the captions—they were architecture students at a Roman university in the magical year of 1968. They seemed to be yelling at someone near the photographer, a policeman or perhaps the dean of the School of Architecture. They were obviously protesting something the architecture department had done (what could it be?) as well as the conservative bent of Italian society in general and, a little bit, the Vietnam War. Jack had not gone into their stated reasons, his Italian not being up to old newspaper clips, but he had found the photographs in a dusty archive in the library of the Roman school (just where Professor Caldwell had suggested they might be), rescued them, blown them up, framed them, and provided the moralizing text: You cannot build justly in an unjust society. He loved the play on "just" and wanted to draw some famous buildings with wavering walls, but in order to move the display a little away from the architectural toward his own special field instead attached a banner titling it *The Landscape of Justice*.

All of the visitors who wandered in headed straight to the photographs, but none of them continued on to the other wall, the Indiana wall, the landscape architecture wall, the wall you had to read. There Jack had framed a memoir written by his old professor. The memoir was about the 1968 protests on the Hoosier campus, protests that had occurred long before Jack's time (he had, in fact, been born in that magical year), protests that had hovered on the edge of violence and might very well have taken down the university in some unspecified way had it not been for the calming speech and brave demeanor of Donald Caldwell, at that time an assistant professor of landscape architecture, newly arrived at the university. Jack had had the manuscript printed in a sophisticated font that suggested both the crowded typewriting of Jack Kerouac's *On the Road* scroll and the revolutionary pronouncements of a mimeograph machine.

It seemed fitting to Jack that no one wanted to read these beautiful pages, but after the first hour he was in a state of anxiety and chagrin as well as bitter understanding: a well-concealed state but a state all the same.

Then, during the second hour of the ordeal, Jack's attention was drawn to a solitary viewer. Reader, rather. An old woman, bent, almost bald, wrinkled but thin and stylishly dressed—like many other visitors—in black. She wore a fur coat that looked like a Rick Owens sable and leaned on a silver-headed cane as she scanned the photographs, then moved in with a device he recognized from the movies as a lorgnette to peer in a nearsighted fashion at the black-framed texts. She looked like Jack's idea of a Roman princess from an old family reduced from its former state of glory but powerful nevertheless, and it suddenly occurred to him that the text was placed so high that no one outside the NBA could make much of the beginning of Donald Caldwell's story. Still, the little old lady was making an effort at the powerful ending, her nose about half an inch from the wall.

The conversation around him had descended to Academy gossip, so now was a good time to excuse himself and attend to his solitary guest. He went up to the wall and stood quietly by her side until she turned her attention away from the text. He then introduced himself as the artist.

"Okay," she said flatly. "Photography versus words, Italy versus America, revolution versus anti-revolution, architecture . . . well, I think I 'get' it, but of course I know something about Donald Caldwell, Savior of the University."

She did not go on, Jack noticed, to venture an opinion, a positive opinion. Certainly her general attitude came across as negative.

"You know Donald? He's one of my best friends. My favorite teacher in graduate school," he heard himself gushing . . . unwisely, he decided. Her flat American accent modified Jack's view of her Roman aristocratic background to one of expatriate industrial wealth. Her stylish black dress might just as easily be a tissue of rags as the latest in haute couture, and the coat, which was far too warm for the weather, was definitely not Rick Owens.

"Well, I know *of* Donald. He married one of my friends from college." The old woman looked at him now, and he was surprised to see that she had been crying, a few weary tears working their way through her wrinkles to her chin.

"You know . . ." He didn't quite know how to put it.

"That she killed herself? Yes, I know that. The alumnae magazine reported her death, and I called up . . . well, not a friend but a classmate, and she said Pamela had killed herself. Shot herself in the head. To make sure."

"It was terrible. I understand Donald came home after class and found her. Apparently she was entering another period of depression and she just couldn't go through it again. Like Virginia Woolf," he added.

"I didn't know he was a revolutionary, ah, anti-revolutionary. All I've heard is he's a closeted gay who fucks his students."

"My God, no!" Jack involuntarily looked around him to make sure no one had heard her. "No, no, no. He's perfectly straightforward about his sexuality, and I don't believe I've ever heard that he slept with anybody."

"An old virgin." She smiled unpleasantly. "But he made sure the university didn't burn down . . . in 1968." Back in the Ice Age, her tone implied. When we could have used the warmth.

"He was a wonderful teacher." Jack felt he could safely defend Donald because no one was listening. "It wasn't a bad thing, his not taking part in the revolution."

"The revolution." She said this in tones that suggested she would add "my ass" but was too well bred.

"He was a really caring, concerned teacher. And this nonsense about his sexuality . . . Let me tell you a story." This was one of Jack's favorite ploys in winning over a hostile audience, not that it had ever appeased any of his disappointed clients. "One day he saw me and Linda" (he nodded at Linda, on the other side of the room, deep in speculation about who was sleeping with whom) "sitting on a bench outside the department office, obviously arguing. And he asked me about her, and I said we were going to get married as soon as I could afford it. But right now I was broke. I couldn't even buy her an engagement ring. And he said, 'Don't worry about that, Jack. It's a small thing. Not worth worrying about.' And he asked me to come up to his office, and he wrote me a check so I could buy her a ring."

"Gag me with a spoon," said the old lady. "Yeccch! Double yecchh!" And before Jack could reply, she was out the door of his studio and into the studio of Gus, the prospective museum designer, where she joined everyone else in her loquacious admiration of his models. Jack noticed that even Linda and her Academy friends were relocating their conversation to Gus's studio so that he alone was left to ponder the importance of design in the tricky world of political action.

*

Several endless hours later the Open Studios closed and dinner was served buffet-style in the back garden of the Academy. For several years, the Academy had hired a chef trained by Alice Waters of Chez Panisse and taken justifiable pride in its cuisine. Nevertheless, many of the guests (Gus the architect among them) had gone on to what Jack assumed were better parties elsewhere because the well-tended garden was almost empty. Night had fallen. No sooner was Jack through the line than he saw the old lady sitting alone in the middle of a group of folding chairs placed near some neatly trimmed bushes, intently eating through a heaped-up plate of food. He watched her wolf it down and noted, with irritation, that she still looked like a lady, even while licking her fingers. "A Napoleon in rags" was the line that sang through his mind.

He went over to the bushes and sat down a few chairs away from her. Out of the corner of his eye he watched Linda take a seat far away near the door to the building. He knew that she and her friends were now talking about the disappointing work of other people in a variety of fields. "Do you mind if I join you?"

"Of course not. I've been expecting you."

"You seem a little hostile to Donald," he ventured.

"Oh, nonsense. I don't even know him. I just knew Pamela. She was in my class in college. We lived on the same floor." And she embarked upon a lengthy memory of Pamela, interspersed with chewing and swallowing, finger-licking, and discreet but unmistakable burps. She was a thorough eater.

Pamela, he gathered, was brilliant and beautiful and rich, a graduate of the fanciest boarding school on the East Coast. Straight A's. Junior Phi Bete. Her parents lived on Park Avenue, and one time when the old lady was staying there with Pamela, it snowed and they spent an unforgettable weekend walking around New York watching the city fill up with white flakes. Pamela gave everyone on their floor a copy of the first Beatles album, and they were sitting in her room singing Beatles songs, waiting until it was time to get on the bus and go to the Harvard–Yale game, when they heard that Kennedy had been shot. Pamela was an art history major, and her freshman year—freshman year!—she wrote a paper about how a painting in the Borghese that everybody thought was just a painting was really part of a missing triptych! A nondescript landscape of barren hills, totally undistinguished, and Pamela had amazingly figured out that it belonged on the left side of some version of *St. Francis Receiving the Stigmata*. Freshman year! Can you imagine the career she was going to have?

The old lady closed with an image, smiling softly at the memory. "She always leaned backward when she walked. Like she was so confident she could just rest on the wind and let it push her wherever she wanted to go."

Although Jack had probably seen Mrs. Caldwell only three or four times in his life, he remembered that detail. She *had* leaned backward when she walked. As if a strong wind was blowing in her face and a little puff might blow her over. He took advantage of this memory to interrupt the old lady's endless monologue and tell her that he too remembered Mrs. Caldwell's strange gait. "She looked like she was putting all her weight on the leash, trying to keep her dog from running away."

"Dog?"

"A black French poodle."

"My favorite breed! Did she take it with her?"

"My God, of course not."

"I just wondered. I did hear somewhere that she'd become a Buddhist. But you never know. I'm sure she had beautiful dogs. Pamela was so beautiful. It only makes sense that she would have fabulous animals. Poodles always remind me . . . Well." Jack could see her decide not to follow that path.

"Well, they looked great together." He followed at a distance.

"I guess, looking back now," the old lady continued, "that the nose thing was the sign of worse to come."

"The nose thing?"

"Well, she had the most beautiful nose. A real beak. It looked like it was designed to sniff out all sorts of scholarly mysteries. You just knew she could look down it and see things nobody else had ever seen before. A wonderful nose for a professor. And then she came back in the fall of senior year, and she'd had it 'done' over the summer. I'll never forget her carrying some cardboard boxes up the stairs, and she had this . . . well, not even straight, but a new sort of snubbed, perky nose. It wasn't the right kind of nose for a brunette, let alone a serious scholar. But what could you say? Lots of girls got their noses done back then."

What was his own nose like? What about Donald Caldwell's? Jack found himself staring at the little old lady's nose. It might have been turned up once upon a time. Now it drooped over the furrows of her upper lip like the Wicked Witch of the West's. He had never seen so many wrinkles. Even her scalp ridged up in little layers like an extension of her eyebrows. "So what happened? I don't remember that she ever wrote anything. Or even taught." He tried to hide his unreasonable surge of pleasure. No wonder Donald relied on his students for intellectual stimulation. "What happened to the great career? I don't know of anything she did besides walk her dog."

"Funny you should ask, you and your little engagement ring. What was it? Half a carat? A quarter of a carat? Do they come that small?" She stared at her empty plate, then looked him over with contempt. Yes, contempt.

He answered. He couldn't help himself. "Quarter."

She let her contempt sink in while she went back to the buffet table and loaded up her plate with seconds. When she got back she ate four chicken wings, licked her fingers, and daintily sucked a few bones before resuming the conversation. While Jack waited, he watched Linda and her friends talking about the essential mediocrity of so many of this year's projects.

"You can't imagine what we girls were like back then. The Seven Sisters had made a real effort to recruit scholarship students. Geographical Distribution, they called it. A few of the smartest of those girls went on to medical school or law school, and the less practical went to graduate school in English or classics or history and then, when they couldn't get jobs, went to law school. But most of the regular girls believed in A Ring By Spring. They'd get engaged by spring of senior year and then married right after graduation in June, and they'd be excused from ever doing anything for the rest of their lives. A ring guaranteed a free ride. It wasn't a metaphor. They really believed it. They could just do what their mothers had done. Nothing. As a result, by fall of senior year, a lot of girls were getting nervous.

"Not everybody. After all, some succeeded. Shelby Forrester from Philadelphia, for example. Shelby got a ring at Thanksgiving, and what a ring it was. Fifteen carats, square-cut. It was so big it had lost its sparkle. It just looked like a big piece of glass or a small ice cube or the kind of ring you'd win at the state fair. But it was real. Shelby lived on our floor, and that December some jolly idiot decided that we would all draw names out of a hat and exchange presents. There was always so much pressure to be congenial, it was easy to get roped into events like that. So . . . we drew each other's names and dutifully bought and wrapped the presents and then sat around a Christmas tree in the downstairs living room drinking some sort of punch and opening our presents, one by one by boring one.

"I got Pamela's name, and I went down to the bookstore and bought her a Dorothy Sayers and wrapped it up in the front page of the *New York Times*, and as luck would have it, she hadn't read it, or at least she was nice enough to say she hadn't. Most of the presents were like that, a mystery or a little scarf or a neat little ashtray. Apparently Shelby was so busy getting engaged to whoever he was that she didn't have time to go buy a present, and since she'd picked the name of one of the least popular girls on the floor, she probably didn't feel a lot of pressure. She just took the insides out of the leather box that her engagement ring had come in—you know, the satin part with the little slot for the ring?—wrapped the box up in a napkin, and gave it to Jane.

"I'll never forget that moment when Jane opened the napkin and pulled out the little leather box. She shook it and then opened it and peered inside in an exaggerated way and said, 'Oh, Cartier! Wow! Cartier! I've always wanted a box from Cartier.' And we all laughed . . . nervously. Jane was from Muncie, Indiana, Geographical Distribution with a vengeance, Geographical Distribution from Hell. She was someone who always worked hard but only got B's, while most of the girls didn't do very much and got C's. And of course everyone admired girls like Pamela who just got A's naturally, and they even liked the girls who worked hard and got A's, but to work hard and get B's seemed . . . well, infra dig, I guess you could call it. But call it what you will, it made Jane look—not dull, really—but goofy. I was in a political science class with her once, and she announced, right in the middle of class, that miscegenation was a better idea than civil rights. She got a C in that class, no matter how hard she worked. She was the kind of girl who slept with all the Yalies she dated, and when the other girls complained, she had the nerve to say, 'Well, what else can you do with them?' That was the sort of thing that made her really unpopular.

"So Jane got the empty red box, and after the party she put it right in the middle of her desk, like it was one of her most prized possessions, and whenever anybody came to visit her—not that they did very often because she was so disliked—she'd pick up her box and show it around and say, 'See, see! This is the box the ring came in. And there's nothing in it anymore. Isn't that amazing?'

"Really, I think more girls dropped by her room and chatted and had a cup of coffee after the party because Shelby's behavior was so embarrassing. It was such a shabby thing to do to somebody who didn't know any better. Although I don't suppose Jane gave a shit. Certainly she didn't care if anyone made fun of her for working hard and making B's—something most of us came to sooner or later, one way or another. And I guess eventually you could say almost everybody had more hands-on experience with miscegenation than civil rights, and certainly in later years a lot of girls came to wonder what else boys were good for. Still, at the time Jane seemed like an idiot, so it was really admirable that some of the girls were at least kind enough to suspect it hurt her feelings, getting the empty box. Pamela was one of those girls, dropping by Jane's room with a fair degree of regularity, having coffee, talking about . . . I don't know. What did they have to talk about?

"In those days we had final exams after we got back from Christmas vacation. It was a good system because it meant that over the holidays you could pretty much do all the assigned reading, and then if you studied really hard during the five days of Study Period, you could do okay on the exams, or at least well enough to get a C. It was about day three of Study Period that the rumor began: Shelby's ring was missing. I don't recall that we thought too much of it, suspecting—silently—that one of the cleaning staff had made off with it and she and it would turn up in good time. I suppose the more savvy of us were wondering how much a fifteen-carat diamond was worth and how someone, particularly someone as sophisticated as Shelby, could just leave it lying around her room. And what would the thief do with it now? Was there a special market for fifteen-carat diamond rings? Whenever she had an audience, Jane, the obnoxious one, would make a big deal of opening the box and looking in and saying, *'Oh, no! It's not here!'* A joke that got old fast. We could only begin to imagine the lives cleaning ladies led, but we did so with earnest hearts, inventing sick children, foreclosed mortgages, boyfriends with drug habits, the desire to go back to high school, and so forth.

"Looking back now, I expect the administration, the dean of students, whatever, spent a pretty uncomfortable week dealing with the local police, but I don't recall anything so demeaning as a room search.

"Finally, near the end of Exam Week, another rumor spread like wildfire around campus. The thief had been found and was currently in the dean's office awaiting the police. Girls rushed back from the library to see the black-and-whites pull up in front of the dormitory. I suppose their presence assured us that the thief was a cleaning lady, but when an ambulance pulled up I think even the dimmest of us began to suspect it was one of our own. When the word about who it was finally wormed its way out, most of the girls cried, whether they knew Pamela or not. I remember Jane cried and cried, although not all the tears in the world could wipe away her snotty, ironic attitude. It was absolutely unbelievable that Pamela—beautiful, brilliant, rich, graduate of the best boarding school on the East Coast—could have stolen Shelby's ring. But almost immediately someone came up with the information that she'd stolen the ring, hocked it at a pawnshop in New York, and given the money to her boyfriend, who was in the theater school at Yale. She didn't think it was fair that a real artist should have to scrounge around for money when a dummy like Shelby had a fifteen-carat engagement ring. I imagine if you'd taken a poll, most of us would have believed the same thing. I don't know where *he* thought the money had come from.

"None of us saw Pamela being escorted to jail, and in fact she didn't actually do any time. They just strapped her onto a stretcher and ferried her out to the ambulance, and while most of us would have agreed with her reasoning to a point, the fact of actually stealing and hocking a fifteen-carat ring—and thinking that somehow she could get away with it—deviated so far from any norm that most of us would have agreed with what happened next. As I understand it she was driven straight from the dorm to a private mental hospital where she spent a year or two or maybe three. Of course Shelby didn't press charges once she got her Cracker Jack prize back.

"At the time we all thought Pamela was just suffering from some senior-year megalomania. Now I understand she was schizophrenic, and it was just the first of a lifetime of breakdowns. But I don't really know firsthand. I sort of lost touch with her at that point. All I know is that she married a gay college professor, bought a Frank Lloyd Wright house, and donated a lot of money to good causes. For that matter I don't even know how she met Donald."

"Oh, he was still in practice at that point," explained Jack. "He did her parents' garden out in the Hamptons."

"Yeccch! Double yecchh!"

"Yeah, I know. *Gag me with a spoon!* But what happened to the rest of you?" Jack asked in a not-entirely-nice tone. "Did the rest of you go on to fulfill your youthful promise? Did you win all the prizes? Did the world fall at your feet in admiration? What happened to Shelby the Engaged? What happened to Jane the Obnoxious? What happened to *you?*"

"Those are long stories." She had finally put aside her second empty plate.

He was openly sarcastic. "If I get you some dessert, will you tell me?"

"Sure," she said. "I'd like one of everything, thank you."

And to the best of his ability he neatly filled a plate with a piece of cake and a scoop of ice cream, a pile of strawberries and something that looked like a small apple pie. But when he got back she was gone, disappeared without a trace into the light of the Academy building or the dark of the Academy gardens.

Linda and her friends had seen him talking with her, but no one noticed where she'd gone, and when he asked around over the next few days, no one could come up with a clear identification for her. The Academy staff was pretty sure they'd seen her around, around the Academy or Trastevere or maybe just around Rome. But everyone was absolutely certain that she had no business attending the Open Studios. Neither a trustee nor a visitor nor a friend, she had wandered in off the street uninvited, blown in by a warm wind, and only good luck had kept her from taking root. Next year they really had to think about beefing up security.

*

During the next few months, as he packed up to go back to Indianapolis, Jack gave a lot of thought to the intruder. Her appearance seemed like a warning about something, although he couldn't figure out what, and eventually he began to think less about her and more about the exact phrasing of those letters to his partners in which he would announce that he was planning to take a few months off and teach at the university spring semester and about the letters next summer announcing that he planned to teach fall semester. He was determined that by the time he was gone, everyone in his office would accept the fact that he was leaving. It was only reasonable to move on, and he knew that he would first become an assistant and then an associate and at last a full professor of landscape architectural history and then the head of his department and the dean of the School of Architecture and the provost of the university—a position he could trade in for the presidency of a small nondenominational college in the southern part of the state.

Still, despite his clear career path, that awkward evening of Open Studios continued to resonate, for a huge, glassy diamond ring frequently made its way into his dreams. Displaced by divorce, discarded by premature death, relegated by that fear of thieves that grows on people as they age, for whatever reason, it has become detached from its owner. Too valuable to give away, too personal to sell, it lies in a safe-deposit box that rests in a vault behind a thick steel door in a bank with classical columns and a pediment in a city on the East Coast. In a metal box ten inches wide, ten inches deep, and two feet long, the ring lies cradled in paper: the birth certificates, baptismal records, report cards, school and college diplomas, marriage licenses, divorce decrees, and property deeds of generation after generation after generation of some perfectly respectable family, the ragged remnants of superior individuals who were really very promising to begin with. And then, as Jack falls into a deeper state of oblivion, the box empties itself out. The certificates, records, reports, diplomas, licenses, degrees, and deeds flutter away, and the ring lies alone in a cold airless dark quiet box. The ring and the box where it ended up.

Meditation XXXI:
On Sustenance

Since there's only one scene in this story and it takes place at the McDonald's out on McGalliard Road in Muncie, Indiana, I'll first kill a little time discussing food. That way, once we get there, we can quickly accustom ourselves to a straightforward act of charity. Therefore, please consider the following an irony-mitigating ramble, rather than an explanatory march, through a subject dear to our hearts.

Some say that Alice Waters is responsible for making Berkeley, California, the epicenter of the current gastronomical earthquake, and while there's exaggeration in that statement, it's undeniable that California is a focus of food culture, thanks in part to Waters—but thanks as well to M. F. K. Fisher and Julia Child and, of course, the wine industry. Much of this focus presumably came into being when Waters (and Fisher) revolted against the saucy complications of French cuisine so pleasantly advocated by Child, in the process transforming Californians into devotees of not only food but also the culture that ripples out from food—magazines, television shows, cookbooks, and high-end restaurants—a culture based on the assumption that food preparation takes just as much consciousness and skill as the practice of, say, painting or sculpting or composing music or writing poetry. Once food was granted this status, it was relatively easy to go on to mythologize the artists and glorify their creations, just as is the case with any other art. And, of course, hidden within this process was the assumption that the art of food depends, like any other art, on the connoisseur who is able to make distinctions imperceptible to most of us. For food to become art, then, requires a sort of silent food snobbishness accompanied by a voiced need for food education. And once food is recognized as an art, it seems only natural to add morality as the last and best ingredient.

Some credit Chez Panisse with the moral seasoning of the current craze, a tang of self-justification derived from the free-speech and anti-war movements as well as from Flower Power, the Grateful Dead, Gay Pride, the commune—all forms of stylistic righteousness that characterized the 1960s and 1970s and that have somehow shifted over the years from preaching how to live to preaching how to eat. Whatever the exact origin, Berkeley's contribution to food morality goes beyond mere flavoring, for the town is also the home of the Berkeley Bowl and the Edible Schoolyard and Michael Pollen, who teaches at the university and authors such straightforwardly moral tracts as *The Omnivore's Dilemma* and *In Defense of Food*. You can almost hear the resounding Yes! as the Berkeley population responds to the rhetorical question lucidly posed in Pollen's books: Isn't gastronomy even more important in a country fighting an epidemic of obesity, which strikes poor people who eat a vitiated diet of fast food contaminated with high-fructose corn syrup and the other dubious products of a food industry represented by an army of lobbyists and subsidized by the federal government? Yes, oh, yes, indeed!

To be fair, many if not most Americans would probably agree with the residents of Berkeley that food preparation is an art and food consumption a worthy cultivation of taste in the broader sense. In fact, the moral-flavored art of food holds sway in the national as well as the local consciousness. There are even foodies, moral foodies, in Indiana. On a recent trip I noticed that my friend the Professor had suddenly become one of them. She's always liked to eat, but everything intensified when she abandoned her usual fields of Shakespeare and Anglo-Saxon poetry to write a modest little article on *The Brothers Karamazov*, interpreting the novel in terms of Smerdyakov's vocation as a cook with an expertise in making soups. Everyone acknowledged that it was a good article, and soon my friend embarked on a long, ambitious book about Jean Anthelme Brillat-Savarin and started calling herself the Professor, not in reference to her employment—teaching English at a local college—but in joking deference to Brillat-Savarin's own self-designation. I think it was really just a trick to stay sane during an exhausting scholarly endeavor, for even though she was an enthusiastic close reader of texts and not a deconstructionist of any sort, my friend was afraid she couldn't do justice to the real Professor's brilliance. She loved his twenty aphorisms and thirty meditations and in her method tried to follow the subtitle of *The Physiology of Taste* (1825)—*Meditations on Transcendental Gastronomy*—that is, she tried to meditate on his text rather than criticize it, to digest it rather than cut it up into little bites. Referring to herself as the Professor was a jocular inoculation against the terrible possibility that she might inadvertently succumb to a different opinion, one quite prevalent even in the midst of our current enthusiasm—the belief that gastronomy is not really an art. Yes, there are still people in the United States, even in Berkeley and Indiana, who wonder if preparing food isn't a relatively easy way to claim the role of artist and eating it a relatively cheap way to label oneself a discriminating connoisseur. These doubters also feel some ambivalence about the righteousness of gastronomy in a world where approximately a sixth of the population—more than a billion people—is "underfed," a euphemism at best. If people don't read novels or enjoy opera, if they loathe the symphony and scorn the art museum, even if they abjure the folk arts, the worst that happens to them is a stunting of their emotional lives. The inability to experience food, good or otherwise, has altogether more drastic consequences. Those who doubt the validity of food as art are also the sort who would question Brillat-Savarin's famous Aphorism IX: "The discovery of a new dish does more for human happiness than the discovery of a star"—although given the larger concerns with health, even these spoilsports probably wouldn't question Aphorism IV: "Tell me what you eat, and I shall tell you what you are." Strange to say, my wary friend the Professor, nervously clinging to her belief in the art of food, came to subscribe wholeheartedly to Aphorism IX and just as wholeheartedly to deny the truth of Aphorism IV, and she came to these divergent readings of the text after she witnessed a simple scene at the McDonald's out on McGalliard Road. There she experienced a dish that "does more for human happiness than the discovery of a star," and there she likewise learned that what we eat may have absolutely nothing to do with what we are.

*

It could not be said that Andy was much of a foodie, even though he'd lived in Berkeley for a decade before he started dating Brenda.

He was aware of eating, or at least of food, because he'd grown up on a farm in Indiana before he escaped to the university of a neighboring state. When he got out of school with a degree in landscape architecture, he worked at a few small offices, then moved to the Bay Area and joined a firm dedicated to the idea of landscape architecture as art. Here he quickly became a partner because he was a field guy, and knowing how a landscape is made, how to do strict working drawings, and how to perform vigilant construction supervision is even more important than usual when a landscape aspires to artistic perfection. As it happened, Andy turned out to be the kind of field guy who demands just that degree of perfection. And he was so good that he quickly became a class unto himself: "You know So-and-so," landscape architects in other offices would say, "he's our Andy." Like the landscape designers he worked for, Andy was also known as something of a martinet, accepting no excuses whatsoever for the most minuscule of mistakes, screaming with exasperation when he came across the shortest of shortcuts or any sort of sloppiness whatsoever. Still, despite his exacting temperament and his Berkeley residence, I don't think he cared very much about food. My guess is that Andy favored frozen dinners and Campbell's soups with occasional forays into simple restaurants like Spenger's Fish Grotto or Brennan's. Or maybe he dined most happily on whatever he picked up at gay bars and bathhouses, although this is pure conjecture. There was something furtive and unfocused in Andy's manner that might spell "closet" or might simply spell "farm boy" in not-so-big-but-oh-so-sophisticated Berkeley.

For one reason or another, Andy surprised everyone when he married Brenda, a secretary at the landscape firm, during the day at any rate. During evenings and vacations she took cooking courses at various Bay Area institutions and as soon as they married spent a year-long internship at Linda's Palace, one of the best of Berkeley's many Chez Panisse offshoots, and then went to Paris for six months to take a course on baking, the very best course of its kind in the world. When she came back to Berkeley she got a job as sous-chef at Café Sublime, another distinguished Chez Panisse spin-off, and somewhere along the line her devotion to food further refined itself to privilege the locally grown. Anyone who has read Pollen on the difference between food from a small farm run in the old way and food from the industrial one-product version can sympathize. Food should be grown in a situation that demands no fertilizer; depends on the ongoing interaction of meat, dairy, vegetable, and fruit; saves energy; and avoids the loss of vitamins by growing in close proximity to its devourers. It seemed perfectly natural for Brenda to believe in food from small-scale local farms—organic goes without saying—although I don't have any evidence about what she actually liked to eat. For Brenda, haute California cuisine, organic and local, was a structural way of looking at the world, and I have no reason to think Andy subscribed to any other belief once Brenda had introduced him to the idea of eating well.

No one was really surprised when Andy announced to the other partners in the firm that he and Brenda were leaving Berkeley to open a restaurant in Gaston, Indiana, the town nearest his parents' farm—a restaurant featuring high-end cuisine created from organic, small-farmed, locally grown products. Of course he would continue to work, returning to Berkeley every other week and flying out to the firm's worldwide projects from Indianapolis rather than San Francisco. One reason no one was surprised was that everyone knew Brenda wanted a restaurant of her own, and it had been widely observed that Brenda's distinguishing physical feature was a set of eyes that bore an amazing resemblance to those of a border collie: A light, light blue infused the irises with the command of the whites and doubled their power. If Brenda wanted a restaurant of her own, what sheep would have the nerve to say her nay? And if Brenda, who grew up in Orange County, wanted to return to some roots for her "local" cuisine, what better place than Andy's hometown? She had recently given birth to their first child, and Andy had widely expressed the opinion that sophisticated Berkeley was a corrupting environment for children.

On their arrival in Delaware County, Andy and Brenda first rented a house in Muncie, the county seat and home of Ball State University with a population of about 70,000; they'd decided it would be easier to live there while they were setting up the restaurant. After all, Gaston (population about 1,000) lacked many amenities besides a high-end restaurant. Its main employment was the industrial farming of tomatoes, although Andy's parents also raised industrial corn. They still lived in the small but solid L-shaped farmhouse Andy had been so ashamed of that he'd quickly leaped into a design field. The catalpa in the weedy front yard and the untamed forsythia bushes were probably responsible for turning him into what he was. Nevertheless, he valued his roots. His parents knew everybody and, most important, respected Brenda's ambitions. To them Brenda seemed so sophisticated and knowledgeable about food that if she wanted to open a restaurant, then it was sure to be a success. And so Locavore, as it was to be called, came to Gaston.

First of all Andy and Brenda bought an old brick building located on Gaston's one-hundred-percent corner, the intersection of a county road and a main street lined with five agriculturally related enterprises, a beautiful building that needed a lot of work. They also bought a four-bedroom brick house, built circa 1890 and once home to Gaston's biggest industrialist during the era when the discovery of natural gas had lured all sorts of businesses to the county. The house was now home to some meth addicts who hadn't managed to make it out to the trailer park on the edge of town, but it still stood apart from the rest of Gaston's housing stock, and this superiority made buying and then restoring it a commonsense investment; for decades now, Andy had been making pretty good money as the firm's field guy, and on the basis of this he took out substantial mortgages on both properties to assure suitable settings for Locavore and its owners.

As for Muncie's opinion about Locavore—well, opinion was mixed. Thirty years of deindustrialization had robbed Muncie of its factories and much of its working class; the university was now the biggest employer in town, and many of the university types tended to approach the Berkeley norm in their opinions about food. Of course some residents belonged to that group castigated by M. F. K. Fisher as "Anglo-Saxon," who take a puritanical stance on food: They did not frequent restaurants, bought their groceries at Marsh's (or the Wal-Mart), and grilled their steaks at home. Another group considered chain restaurants sufficient for their needs. But for the citizens of Muncie who regularly dined out, a new restaurant of any sort came as a welcome reprieve from Bessie Sue's, which was six or seven years old at this point. Dave, a native of a small town in the southern part of the state, had graduated from Ball State with a degree in business and spent fifteen years working in various local food-service jobs, including a stint at the Holiday Inn. Eventually he hooked up with the handsome Ray, who was fresh from a closet where he had managed several businesses, including the lumber yard and the bottling company belonging to his then father-in-law. Together Dave and Ray convinced a local lawyer to put up some money so they could rent—and eventually buy—a small brick building that had once been the drugstore on Muncie's main drag, at this point by and large deserted for the mall out on McGalliard

Road. They furnished the place with tables and chairs from Goodwill, Indianapolis antiques stores, and the attics of friends; these were also the sources of the mismatched china, the tinny silverware, the clouded mirrors, and—a real find!—several large gold-framed Archimboldo prints. They bought glasses and cookware on credit. And they named the restaurant after Dave's grandmother, who had run a tearoom back in Boonville.

After fifteen years in the food business, Dave knew what people wanted to eat, and he devised a menu that included thick, aromatic onion soup (concocted of canned bouillon, fried onion slices, and Velveeta); a wedge of iceberg lettuce served with bottled blue-cheese or Thousand Island dressing; main courses of chicken smothered in raspberry jam, a big filet, a small filet, fish of various kinds (flown in more or less daily), and spinach ravioli (mass-produced by a company outside Denver); and, for dessert, a changing array of pies and cakes from the kitchen of Ray's cousin Cora, who liked to bake. He bought a lot of wine from a reliable supplier, and when Orchard, the other fancy restaurant in Muncie, went out of business, its owner, a successful cartoonist, gave his extensive cellar to Dave as a sort of congratulatory present to himself for getting out of the restaurant business.

You didn't have to be Alice Waters to know that Bessie Sue's cuisine was ridiculous. It was modeled, Dave and Ray claimed, on Dave's grandmother's menus, but despite the aura of family history, everyone knew it was really just cheap ingredients cooked up by somebody without much skill. And yet it tasted pretty good, and Dave and Ray were at Bessie Sue's all the time, and there was a piano player on weekends, and the restaurant was an overnight success, a place where people could go and eat as they had once eaten at Orchard or, before that, at Slim's (run by two gay guys who'd retired to Florida sometime in the 1990s). On any given night at Bessie Sue's you might find the head of the anthropology department and her girlfriend, the president of the bank and her husband, the heads of all the social-service agencies, the last heir of the Ball Brothers' canning-jar empire and the new president of the Ball Foundation, various university administrators, my friend the Professor, four or five doctors, any number of lawyers and financial managers, the head of the insurance company, the famous architect (or sculptor or writer or politician) who was giving a lecture at the university, and his or her departmental hosts. Versions of this crowd also came for lunch, seeing each other noon after noon and night after night, and they always had a good time, not least because a restaurant run by two gay guys was a place in Muncie where you could let your hair down a little.

Dave cleverly hired a bartender and a waitstaff from the gay community; depending on your waiter, you could catch up on Muncie's dress-designing, easel-painting, crafts-producing, home-decorating, flower-arranging, or art-glass scene, information heavily larded with detailed gossip. Ray was pretty conservative, but he knew absolutely everybody from managing the lumberyard and the bottling company, and Dave could be as outrageous as the occasion called for. And, really, everyone liked gay guys, especially if they acted ironic about their gayness and flaunted it, even while they were faithful to each other and thriftily bought real estate and invested in beautiful old cars, including a 1939 Mercury that they exhibited every year at Fairmont's James Dean Festival. They kissed everybody on the lips, sat at their tables and discussed so-and-so's well-deserved bankruptcy and how so-and-so was cooking the books and who was doing what with whom, and, depending on the tastes of the diner, shared cell-phone photographs of a cow sucking a long, long dick or engaged in earnest discussions about Academy Award contenders. Ray even appeared in a Civic Theater production, to universal delight, and a few years before Brenda and Andy moved to town the Restaurant Boys, as they called themselves, instituted a summer tour—the Senior Trip—with themselves in charge of ten faithful customers sailing down the Rhine or the Mississippi or even along the Yellow River. The one thing Dave and Ray never did was drink with the customers—a long story, that, and one to relate on another occasion.

So what did Dave and Ray think about Andy and Brenda and Locavore? For within days of moving into their Muncie rental Brenda and Andy had dropped in for dinner at the nonlocal, nonorganic Bessie Sue's, mostly because they were lonely, despite the presence of Andy's family ten miles away, but also because they wanted to get to know Locavore's future customers. Of course their visits grew less frequent after Brenda got pregnant again and preparations for Locavore began in earnest. Not surprisingly, Dave and Ray took an immediate liking to good old weak-willed gray-skinned ex-farm-boy obsessive-compulsive-professional Andy, perhaps because they recognized themselves in him, and they accompanied this affection with a genial loathing of Brenda and a quasi-ironic nattering about Locavore itself because they thought it neither seemly to denigrate the opposition nor intelligent to wax enthusiastic.

After the birth of Andy and Brenda's second daughter, Locavore moved more energetically toward its opening. And what was the restaurant like? Well, for one thing, the old brick building, once a grocery store, had been beautifully redone. Its stamped-tin ceiling glowed, as did its new hardwood floors, white walls, white china, stainless-steel cooking and eating utensils, and artfully simple fluorescent lighting. Its white linen tablecloths and napkins were finely woven and spotless. A glass wall opened into the kitchen so you could watch your food being prepared. And it was local food. For more than a year Brenda busily organized the acquisition of meat and dairy from local sources frequently associated with the nearby Amish community or at least no farther away than Fort Wayne or Indianapolis or, at the remotest, Chicago. She successfully convinced local farm families, also frequently Amish, to produce fruits and vegetables (which they could do year-round thanks to some barely standing but usable greenhouses). Fish was challenging and wine a problem, although not so insurmountable as you might think, for thanks to a vine-growing fad in the south of the state, local, or localish, wine began to arrive at Locavore, necessitating the purchase of an expensive, politically complicated liquor license. Brenda effectively used her border-collie eyes to train an inexperienced group of workers who were anxious for employment, while she continued to confirm, day after day, the arrangements with those farmers who were to supply her with everything she had to cook. Or have the cook cook, because she almost immediately realized that she would have to spend all her time acquiring ingredients in all seasons of the year and getting them delivered or picking them up herself and deciding what the menu could be, given what she'd been able to fetch in the intervals between keeping the books and trying to weasel more loans out of Farmers Union and looking for help who still had all their teeth and keeping a close eye on them and figuring out salaries and taxes. She was lucky to find Marty, a manageable drunk who'd learned to cook at Bessie Sue's. At last all the arrangements were made, and Locavore opened to rave reviews in the Muncie, Indianapolis, Fort Wayne, and even Chicago newspapers.

And then it failed. No matter its culinary and moral strengths, Locavore was just too far out in the country to attract customers. Of course Dave and Ray's customers had immediately deserted Bessie

Sue's, rushed out to Locavore, eaten their fill, waxed eloquent about Locavore's superiority, sipped the local wines, and, after a few visits, never returned. Because? Not only was it a long drive back to town at the end of an evening of fun, but . . . it actually wasn't very much fun to begin with. No chattering gay guys with the latest gossip and funny pictures on their phones. No waitstaff conversant with the latest in the arts. No gusto, when you got right down to it. There was food, and superior food at that, but there was nothing at Locavore to inspire a passionate desire to eat.

The restaurant quickly closed, but the building didn't sell quickly, and neither did the ridiculously expensive liquor license or the old brick mansion. Brenda and Andy and the girls moved in with Andy's parents, into the old bedroom he'd deserted so many years before, and although Andy struggled to get their finances in order, they went bankrupt with spectacular abruptness. And then one afternoon when Brenda was at Farmers Union bravely trying to arrange yet another loan, she collapsed in the lobby from what turned out to be a thoroughly obliterating stroke. As soon as she stabilized, Andy put her in Epworth, a Muncie nursing home affiliated with the Methodist church, and paid close attention to her care. Day and night he sat at her bedside, giving up on the finances and leaving the girls to his parents. He still sporadically visited the Berkeley office, but he couldn't go on the road anymore; he couldn't concentrate; he couldn't bring himself to scream about careless construction drawings and inadequate execution. For more than a year he sat at Brenda's bedside, hopeful about her recovery, her improvement, just a little improvement. But then she rejected the feeding tube and, independent of his wishes or her own, quickly died.

In Meditation XXVI, Brillat-Savarin reminds us that death is a law, not a punishment—*Omnia mors poscit; lex est, non poena, perire*—and of all his thoughts, this may well be the wisest as well as the hardest for us to appreciate, not least because it lies so far beyond the art of gastronomy and the morality of food. Andy and Brenda did everything right when they set up Locavore, an undeniable fact. Five years after Brenda's death, local food grows all over the county, and there are several organic grocery stores, three in small towns like Gaston and one in downtown Muncie itself. There's even a farmers' market every Saturday, sponsored by the Cultural Arts Center. In terms of food, then, Andy and Brenda did everything right, yet nothing worked out for them. Although the Professor wanted to make some sense of this—because of course, like everyone else in town, she'd heard about it all in great detail at Bessie Sue's—what came to her mind that day at McDonald's was a baffling message, impenetrable yet unforgettable. She felt like a prophetess at Delphi, sniffing the volcanic fumes from a fissure in the rocks and uttering a profound riddle that promised future wisdom but that she herself did not understand. She watched the scene at McDonald's. Letting down her guard, she sniffed the greasy air, and a message erupted into her mind: *God eats the world*. She had absolutely no idea what that message meant.

*

The nursing home was only a few blocks from a corner of McGalliard Road where there were a couple of bars and a McDonald's, and Andy walked over not really paying attention to where he was going but knowing once he got to the corner that if he went into a bar, he'd never leave. There would be a lot to do tomorrow, and even though it was only five in the afternoon and tomorrow was a long way off, Andy was a conscientious person. He was the one who had to cope with any tomorrow, and so he must refuse to go into one of the bars. If you had looked down from Heaven in the past, you'd most likely have seen him on a landscape site, bent over, scrutinizing construction, searching closely for mistakes, and ready to stick it to the contractor. But if you looked down from Heaven now, you'd see him, dry-eyed, gray-faced, hunched over his misery, holding it to his chest, and dazed with the vision of a mistake someone was surely responsible for, a mistake no one could put right, scurrying along McGalliard Road and dreading tomorrow.

He had to go somewhere. He couldn't stand the thought of driving back to Gaston. Maybe he should rest for a few minutes at McDonald's and think about what to do next. There is nothing subtle about comeuppance, as anyone who might be looking down from Heaven knows. He stood at the edge of the McDonald's parking lot, trying to make up his mind whether to go in and then starting across and speeding up a little because of the fat black girl who stood there holding the door for him, patiently waiting for him and holding the door, not smiling or saying hello, just holding the door open until he made his way across the parking lot and entered, then going back to her table and watching him stare at the gaudy photographs of food displayed above the counter. She looked familiar to Andy. Did she work at the nursing home? She wasn't in uniform, but maybe she'd changed into civilian gear when her shift was over. That was one thing he liked about Epworth: Real Americans worked there, not like the nursing homes in Berkeley, where he'd heard the workers were all Eritreans, Ethiopians, and Somalians.

I'll just get a Coke, a Diet Coke, and then I'll leave, he promised himself, or someone else, someone looking down from Heaven. But when the kid asked him what he'd have, he just kept staring at the pictures of food above the counter and ordered nothing: 20 Chicken McNuggets, Big Mac, Quarter Pounder, Double Quarter Pounder, Two Cheeseburgers, Ranch BLT, Southern Style Chicken, Angus Deluxe. All the sandwiches were bigger than the bun, cheese dripping over the edge of the meat as a result of poor planning? Poor execution? The sheer difficulty of resting a square on a circle? And the fries in a red cardboard carton with golden arches on the side, a carton showing you where you were, as if one of McDonald's' greatest concerns was locating you in reality: You Are Here, Right Here. He remembered Brenda and wondered if he looked strange when he was seen from somewhere up above, standing in front of a McDonald's counter, staring with amazement at pictures as if he'd never seen fast food before, wondering if they were photographs of real food or photographs of plaster models made to look like food, taking an interest in the pictures only because under Brenda's tutelage he'd gotten into the habit of carefully thinking about everything that went into his mouth. There was no one else in the place, just two women, one of them the black girl who'd held the door for him and looked familiar, and he thought, without thinking, what a shame it was that she was fat. Like so many African Americans who ate this shit every day. It was one more hangover from slavery, as Brenda used to explain, making them eat this shit, and then she'd go on and on about the Edible Schoolyard and how it was going to change how blacks ate and make them less liable to poverty, bad schools, and criminal activity. Behind him he could feel the fat girl watching him as he stared at the pictures of fast food.

Over in a corner, ignored by Andy, sat the Professor. She also watched Andy stand transfixed by the images above the counter.

A few days earlier someone had told Andy that the tube wasn't working, and though he hadn't known exactly what that meant, he didn't ask. It wasn't like a construction site where he was in charge of finding mistakes and putting them right. It was *their* job. He was sure they could fix it, whatever it was. "Fix it," he'd said to the usual idiots. They'd gotten into the habit over the past year of announcing everything in a tone of voice suggesting that whatever it was meant the End, as if they were giving him the last little bit of bad news, bad news that would make him pull the plug, although they never said, "Pull the plug."

"Fix it," he'd said, just as he'd said times without number to hundreds of contractors: It isn't right. Fix it. A few months back, one massage therapist had told him she was sure Brenda was paying attention; Brenda knew when someone was massaging her legs, a sign that things were getting better. But the massage therapist had left. For a better job, they said. Or she'd been fired for telling him better news than they wanted told to someone they hoped would soon take upon himself the responsibility for pulling the plug.

The fat black girl was actually the assistant to Mrs. Wooster, head of Epworth, and it was not surprising that Andy didn't recognize her because Shauna was definitely behind the scenes. She knew about Andy because it was her business to know about everything, and even though she'd heard the news about Brenda just before she'd left for the day, she was surprised to see Andy standing at the edge of the parking lot, staring tentatively at the restaurant like a lost soul assessing the Gates of Hell. She had gotten into the habit of dropping into McDonald's twice a week for dinner between work and heading off for her night class at Ball State, where she was getting a master's degree in business administration. Her two children stayed with her mother on the nights she had classes, and Shauna was grateful to her mother— and also grateful for having an hour to herself to eat her favorite meal, something she could never tell her mother, who was a wonderful cook and whose feelings would be hurt if she knew how Shauna felt about Big Macs. Shauna was a dutiful person, careful of others' feelings and grateful for every chance that came her way, apt in fact to be grateful for things she brought about herself. For example, she was particularly grateful for her job at Epworth with Mrs. Wooster, who was the smartest person she had ever known.

Mrs. Wooster was famous for saying she wanted Epworth to provide patients with a hotel-like experience. It should not smell like a nursing home. It should not look like a nursing home. She took particular pride in the dining room, in its beautiful curtains and elegant tablecloths and food that everyone loved, patients and staff alike, because they'd eaten it their whole lives. Louise, the cook, was terrific at everything, but she specialized in Jell-O salads (coleslaw in lime, peaches in orange), and Shauna rolled them through her mind as she ate her Big Mac. In some magic way the thought of them made the Big Mac taste even better than usual. Louise was an artist, everyone agreed, and a big selling point for Epworth. People, especially old, sick people, liked to eat the food they'd grown up with, and their prosperous children liked to see them eat it and, when they came to visit their parents, liked to eat it themselves because it reminded them of how far beyond Muncie they'd progressed. Mrs. Wooster set up two little private dining rooms so children could come have meals with their parents and see how well they were being taken care of, and Shauna saw this with her own eyes because like all the office staff she had one meal a day in the dining room, in her case lunch with a table of old ladies who had to be fed, herself taking a hand with the feeding even though it was probably against some state law. The old people loved Shauna because so many of them had been fed by Negroes when they were little. It was a racist response, Shauna recognized, but she forgave because they were now so very, very old. And as she'd sat there in McDonald's eating her Big Mac, she'd been thinking, not without a certain residual bitterness, about these old ladies, and then she'd looked out the window, and there was Andy standing at the edge of the parking lot.

Shauna now kept her eye on Andy. As he stared up at the pictures, a restaurant came to his mind, a restaurant he'd entirely forgotten about, the restaurant at the Hotel Roberts, Muncie's finest hotel when he was growing up. He remembered it as dark and red and candlelit, with white tablecloths and cloth napkins and heavy silver with someone's initials on the handles. He'd probably gone only two or three times, when his father's sister had driven down to Gaston for a visit. She'd escaped to Chicago and thought nothing of inviting the four of them, Andy, his parents, and his brother, to drive into Muncie and eat at the Roberts. Whatever had happened to the restaurant at the Hotel Roberts? He'd forgotten all about it, and now he realized that for some reason or other it had failed.

Finally Shauna couldn't stand it any longer. She went up to the counter and took Andy's arm and guided him to a table, and then she went back to the counter and ordered a Big Mac with fries and a Coke. And when it was ready she took the order over to him, explained that she worked at Epworth, she'd heard the news, and she was sorry, and then went back to her own table. The Professor and Shauna watched Andy eat the Big Mac bite by bite as he wondered if Brenda was looking down on him from Heaven, where there is no eating and drinking, looking down on him and forgiving him and admitting in some way that there were things more important than food. When he'd finished his Big Mac and the Coke—but not the fries—he went over to Shauna's table, said thank you, and left.

The Professor watched the scene and ate her Big Mac and every one of her fries and drank all of her real Coke, a special treat, her present to herself, better than anything Bessie Sue's and Locavore had to offer, and she thought about the Berkeley Bowl, where she had never been. She imagined Andy and Brenda going to the Berkeley Bowl to buy their groceries for the week, lugging their baby along in a backpack and pushing their cart through the aisles and staring critically at the boxes, piles, and pyramids of fruits and vegetables, unfathomable in their abundance, seven kinds of red potatoes and even more purple ones and about forty sorts of apples and every version of orange and lemon you could imagine, globes of yellow, orange, and green in a variety of shades and sizes, each arranged in its appropriate location. She saw that Andy and Brenda were a lot like those beautiful fruits and vegetables, beautiful fruits and vegetables waiting to be bought and eaten by equally beautiful people, shoppers and eaters as beautiful as Andy and Brenda, so beautiful that the Angel of Good Eating could look down from Heaven and compare them, one to another, and choose the best. Andy and Brenda would be chosen: Just from looking at them anyone could tell they were industrious, keen planners, sharp-eyed enthusiasts, not afraid to do what others were afraid to even think about doing, the best of their kind, the best of a pile of others who also did not believe in eating foods contaminated by chemicals and shipped from the far reaches of the globe, who believed in buying simple, real food and transforming it into something almost unimaginably good, unimaginable yet reminiscent of some ideal meal not eaten at your kitchen table but somewhere civilized beyond your dreams, the best restaurant in the universe. She saw this, and a new aphorism, Aphorism XXI, exploded in her head: *God eats the world.*

*

As a final note, the Professor learned a few months later that some things turned out all right for Andy. For one thing he got fired. The landscape architecture firm wasn't getting much business selling its craft as art, and as happens so frequently in the design world, one stylistic ideal, Art, was happily replaced by another—in this case, Sustainability. Suddenly what the firm was selling was not beautiful landscapes but ecologically conscientious landscapes that sustained themselves. Nobody really understood what this meant, but the Client Class agreed it wanted to buy only Sustainable Landscapes. And so with Art Landscapes out of favor, a great field guy like Andy was less necessary, although to tell the truth, after what he'd been through he wasn't a very good field guy anymore, so the firm fired him. But since he was a partner, even a lousy one at this point, they had to pay a goodly sum to get rid of him, and this turned out to be enough money for him to get more or less out of debt and move the girls to Indianapolis, where he got a job with a little landscape office that was doing pretty well selling the Hoosier version of Sustainability. A few months later, the Professor heard about this from Dave when she took him out to McDonald's for his absolutely-secret-birthday-celebration lunch, and she thought, Okay, well, okay, *God eats the world in little bites.* She understood her own prophesy, and that was a sign to her. No longer the Professor, she went home, threw away everything she'd written on Brillat-Savarin, and sat down to crank out yet another little article on *Twelfth Night*, a play about the gender-bending survivors of a shipwreck who invade a peaceful town to its ultimate advantage.

Atlas Shrugging

You've got to be kidding, was Phyllis's predictable response. Wasn't it written for idiots? A work of science fiction, *The Road* plus *Utopia*, with every archconservative idea exhaustively explained and then amplified with pages and pages of highly unlikely dialogue? A book usually read by teenaged boys to strengthen them for manhood, so wouldn't it prove to be something of an ordeal for two sophisticated ladies in their late sixties, elegantly educated, widely traveled, exhaustively well-read?

Nevertheless, once the book came up, they knew they had to read it.

Every summer Rachel flew out to California to spend a few weeks with Phyllis, her friend from graduate school, and this year they'd taken the occasion to drive up to Trinidad to visit Rachel's cousin Lucinda, whom she hadn't seen for a long time. Lucinda had recently moved out of assisted living into an apartment with elaborate private arrangements, having rediscovered at the age of eighty that servants are easier to manage than institutional caretakers because they have to do what you tell them since, after all, you're paying their salaries. It was on the drive back down to Mendocino that the book came up—along with their realization that they'd have to read it now. And since they knew it would be awful, they took the same precautions they'd taken when faced with difficult assignments in graduate school, an experience from which both of them had failed to profit, each in her own way, although they were still devoted, now as then, to the notion that art has to be skillful to work. But Dostoevsky it wasn't.

Back in the District of Columbia, Rachel was still teaching at the Episcopalian girls school she had despised for twenty-five years, so once the semester began, she made herself read one chapter a day, dutifully if not passionately, just as if Harold Bloom himself had enthusiastically assigned it for class and she just couldn't let him down. Since there were thirty chapters in the book, she started promptly on October 1 and finished up sometime in the early morning of Halloween, a completion date that struck her as somehow suitable. By contrast, Phyllis, in Mendocino, who hadn't retired because she'd never had a job and had never worried much in graduate school about completing assignments because she'd always felt she had better things to do, just crawled into bed every night about ten with a big glass of wine—fuck you, Mr. Wimsatt—and read until she could read no more. And while this meant that she got stuck about five chapters in, she picked it up again in June and managed to finish by the beginning of September, when Rachel, now happily retired, flew out for her next visit. Once in a while Phyllis would even fall into liking the book, the result of a temperament that tended to take an optimistic or at least a positively exploitative view of failure, even those of others. In this fashion the two friends—who'd been inseparably united by their inability to succeed in graduate school—felt they'd done justice to the problem that had arisen on last summer's drive back from Trinidad.

You've got to be kidding, was what Phyllis had said on the drive back. They inched along the coast highway, a road too narrow for tankers, they'd been told, which was why gas was so expensive in Trinidad, a narrow path weaseling its way up and down, back and forth between the encroaching roots of redwoods as if trying to escape responsibility for arriving anywhere, then crawling in tight curves past hidden fields of marijuana plants before it straightened itself out for a brief run along a steep cliff flanked on one side by the dark-gray fog-enshrouded sea and on the other by one-story towns full of aging hippies and gaps in the architecture, a region deserted when the lumber industry moved on, leaving behind it lots of trees but not much else. Driving up to Trinidad, they'd exhausted the topic of decaying buildings and extensive homelessness—the folks camping out in the woods behind Phyllis's house, the ragged youths and their pathetic dogs strategically positioned in front of Mendosa's grocery store—and now, on their way back, once they had discussed the beat-up trailers in the parking lot of Lucinda's new, presumably fancy condominium, Rachel was afraid Phyllis would get sick of driving and ask her to take over. And so it seemed wise to tell a diverting tale that would keep Phyllis's mind away from the question of why anyone closely related to Rachel and prosperous, indeed rich, would ever choose to live out her final years in a dreary village on the north coast of California, whether in assisted living or that suspiciously marginal condominium, all on her own except for paid servants. No. That was not the story, or not the story to be told right now. For some reason the friends couldn't fall into their usual chatter, Rachel complaining about everybody she taught and everybody she taught with and Phyllis bitching about her current husband, just as she'd bitched over the years about a long string of men Rachel could never quite keep straight. And always, always literature. It was conceivable that since Rachel was retiring next June, she'd felt a sudden gush of appreciation for her fellow teachers, and perhaps Phyllis was so old she'd lost interest in men, and maybe they hadn't read anything good or terrible for months. In any case they couldn't find quite the right conversational topic, and so Rachel told Phyllis the story of Ilse and assisted living.

Ilse was in her late seventies, some ten years older than Rachel and Phyllis. Tall, spare, and white-haired, she was always expensively and fashionably dressed and for most of her professional life had been the office manager of a large Washington law firm with an extensive Eastern European and Far Eastern clientele. She owned a condominium with a swimming pool Rachel had taken advantage of for several decades. She was a theater devotee (which was how Rachel had originally met her, in the lobby at the Arena Stage chatting up two young actors), but it was now harder and harder to convince her that going to the theater would still be fun and safe, Rachel actually having to talk her into going to the theater when she always said she'd have been an actress if only things had been different.

Yes, Rachel's story about Ilse was staged as a complaint about Ilse's growing old and giving up and not making an effort. She had sold her condominium (with the pool) and moved into an assisted-living facility, not the one she'd wanted to go to—the one near Sibley Hospital where Washington's well-to-do retired in comfort and style—but a dismal institution out in the Maryland suburbs. Pretty much the sort of place you vowed you'd never go and yet eventually did because it was if not cheap at least not ridiculously expensive and Ilse had discovered that a decent life in old age required a lot more money than she'd ever imagined when she was taking all those marvelous trips Rachel had envied so much over the years. Given assisted-living establishments,

Rachel could see why her cousin had moved into that ugly servant-intensive apartment in Trinidad, but she left that out of the story for fear of further irritating an already irritated Phyllis, who plowed on, looking neither to left (abandoned town) nor right (fog-enshrouded ocean) and possibly wondering why she had driven Rachel up to see this awful cousin, who'd married the Marhofer Wiener heir of Muncie, Indiana, and then lost him to someone else along with apparently all of her common sense. If you wanted to live swaddled in care, why not live in Manhattan, where the help lead interesting lives they can tell you about while they fix your lunch? Why huddle in Trinidad like a big, white, poisonous toad in a tiny, muddy hole? Rachel had no idea where she'd go after she retired, no desires, really, and Phyllis, committed to Mendocino by her current husband's avaricious and totally boring real estate concerns, never gave the future a thought.

Ilse's situation, Rachel began, was particularly sad because Ilse had been sure, right up to the day she moved into the institution out in Maryland, that Andrei would pick up the tab for the pricier establishment near Sibley Hospital and then—

Andrei? That caught Phyllis's attention. A man's name. Have I missed something? Who is Andrei?

Well, of course, she'd missed the whole story, one of Phyllis's most irritating traits. She'd spent her whole life wrapped up in her own thoughts and missed almost everything. Rachel could still see her falling asleep in Shakespeare. Although Rachel could now tell her who Andrei was with the assurance of having her attention safely diverted from ex–Mrs. Marhofer Wiener.

Andrei had been Ilse's—

Remind me, Phyllis ventured. Who is Ilse? I mean, I know you always go to plays with her, but who *is* she?

The story of Ilse, a good story to tell an easily distracted and irritated friend while driving through a world that looked as if it had been recently visited by a neutron bomb. Ilse had been born in Berlin around 1930. Her mother died when she was very young, and when her father was drafted in the early years of the war, he made arrangements for Ilse to live with old friends he'd worked with in some Berlin bureaucracy—a couple with enough room in their apartment for a toddler, who in the course of the war grew up to be a beauty the friend found no trouble marrying after his wife died.

No, Rachel answered the question Phyllis hadn't quite managed to formulate, no, the friend was not a child molester, or at least not that Ilse had ever mentioned. Just someone who was lonely in war-devastated Berlin and saw in Ilse a meaningful, if slightly underage, consolation. Her father was dead by then, somewhere in Russia, later scene of much of this story, and as far as Phyllis knew, Ilse felt she was lucky to have captured the sexual affection of a middle-aged man who kept food of sorts on the table and a roof, even if damaged, over her head until several years after the end of the war, when she met her second (maybe first legal) husband, Fred, who was in the United States Air Force and after Berlin was stationed—believe it or not—in the very same Trinidad they'd left only a few hours ago, even though it seemed like more than a few.

That must have been pretty bleak even after Berlin, Phyllis commented, a little commercial-fishing village with a military base attached. She was nice enough not to say more.

But it was a great place to learn English, Rachel enthusiastically countered. Ilse put English to good use when Fred was transferred to some base outside Washington. Langley, maybe. In fact, Ilse almost immediately got the job at the international law firm where she stayed for the next forty years because she could speak German, Polish, Czech, French, Italian, English, and even more than a little Russian. Rachel wasn't quite sure what the law firm specialized in or why it was headquartered in D.C. as opposed to, say, Hong Kong, but she knew Ilse was valued for her linguistic abilities. Although they never had any children, she stayed happily married to Fred, who died around 1980, and she got his military pension, so she had plenty of money to take those thrice-yearly vacations Rachel had envied so much: sightseeing trips to Europe, especially Germany, and eventually Hungary, Austria, Czechoslovakia and, of course, Russia. Fred was a good provider, first in Berlin, then in Trinidad, next in Washington, and finally, after his death, spiritual host of an extensive travel agenda.

It was on a wonderful trip to Russia in 1990 that Ilse met Andrei. In fact, he drove the tour bus. A tall, thin, dark young man she could see had ambitions and intelligence far above his lot in life, a young man meant for better things. After all, she'd met a lot of young men at the law firm, so she knew potential when she saw it. He even spoke German and English, although she told Rachel she could never figure out where he'd picked them up. She told Rachel how Andrei had made a beeline for her right at the airport, and she'd immediately liked him a lot more than anyone else on the tour, and that's how they became friends, exchanging numerous letters over the next year. By the time she went back to Moscow the following summer, Andrei had left the tour company and was driving a taxi, which Ilse in effect hired for the duration of her stay. But when she returned the year after that, Andrei was no longer available or indeed around, having transformed himself into one of those billionaire entrepreneurs who picked up the leavings when the old Soviet system fell apart, showing his cleverness by embracing the idea of a Russia that could forge an energetic free-enterprise system to replace the paralytic nonsense of Communism, clever enough that, driving buses and taxis, he'd nevertheless some-how managed to tap into the system of Putin-directed insiders who knew how to acquire the leavings, although Rachel couldn't quite remember—perhaps because Ilse didn't know or had failed to tell her—his particular field of endeavor. Steel? Copper? Electrical generators? Railroads? But Phyllis knew what she meant: a billion-aire entrepreneur. You've seen photographs of them in the paper in recent years, buying Western movie companies and basketball teams, multimillion-dollar mansions in Paris and New York City, islands in Greece, famous racehorses, and then, just for the fun of it, almost as if they couldn't help themselves, just as if they couldn't stand the bore-dom of free-market achievement, suing each other or getting involved in politics and heading off to jail after falling out with Putin, who blondly, blandly turned the key in the lock, unless they'd been wise enough to move their money and themselves out of Russia.

Andrei and Ilse kept in touch over the next few years with an exchange of letters, more of which no doubt came from Ilse than from Andrei. And yet he was clearly concerned about her, and one time—maybe her seventieth birthday, maybe her retirement party—sent her a big check, which she spent on a new car she eventually gave to a needy young actor when she went into the undesirable assisted-living establishment out in Maryland. But in spite of the unbelievable con-dominium in New York, Andrei never seemed to come to the United States or even London, haunt of so many of those guys during the boom. And even though Ilse returned to Russia several times, she never actually saw him again, the movement from tour-bus/taxi driver to billionaire necessitating a life of security and secrecy that did not allow visits from tall, multilingual, charming, white-haired American office managers of international law firms, even if she was the one who, in a sense, had given him his start in the first place, the one who was, after all, responsible for his success. And yet Ilse was awfully disappointed when she wrote Andrei a long letter explaining her assisted-living options, near Sibley Hospital or out in the Maryland suburbs, complete with a list of costs and relative benefits . . . and received no answer. Mail being what it might be in Russia, given what it was like here, she sent the letter again several times before she had to sign in at the less-desirable option.

Okay, back up, commanded Phyllis. I don't really see why she'd expect him to pick up her tab at a home. I mean, one big check, or a check big enough for a new car, that's one thing. But why would she expect him to take care of her for the rest of her life? She met him on a tour, for God's sake! He drove the bus! Next year he drove the taxi! Give me a break!

Well, she was beautiful. Maybe I forgot to tell you how beautiful she was. Without beauty she'd never have survived the war, let alone gotten to America.

Okay, beautiful. But she must have been thirty years older than this Andrei. It wasn't sex, was it? It wasn't love. It doesn't seem to me like he owed her anything at all, protested Phyllis. In fact I don't see why he was so interested in her in the first place. So why did she expect him to pay for her assisted living? I don't get it. What do you mean she was the one who gave him his start? How was she responsible for his success? What did she have to do with it?

I think, Rachel explained, it was on that second trip, when he drove her all over Moscow in his taxi. It was then that she gave him the present that changed the direction of his life forever, the present that transformed him from a taxi driver into a billionaire entrepreneur.

So, what did she give him?

A book. Rachel was sure Phyllis had never read it. And then she uttered the title.

You've got to be kidding! Phyllis was so shocked she all but pulled over onto the edge of the road, hindered in large part because there wasn't any edge, just road and ditch and cliff and dark-gray fog-enshrouded sea.

*

The next year the friends had done their reading, and for once even Phyllis was prepared for class discussion. She even had a copy of the book with lots of underlining and stickies on passages that proved her points. So early in the morning of the second of September, she picked Rachel up at the airport, and they headed off to Trinidad, where Lucinda was back in assisted living, having discovered the difficulty of managing help when you don't have the use of your legs, no matter what you pay them. Both Rachel and Phyllis were prepared to find the assisted-living/nursing home awful, even though there apparently wasn't a better one in Trinidad, and assured themselves, just as if they were taking an elementary school field trip to the dairy farm or the fire station, that once they saw Trinidad's best they would be able to see why it had made so much difference to Ilse where she went, the luxurious home near Sibley Hospital that she couldn't afford or the awful place out in the Maryland suburbs where she ended up. Rachel had been out to visit her five or six times, and it wasn't so much that it was awful as that it was easy to imagine someplace much, much better if only the shirking Andrei had accepted his duty and agreed to pay the bills.

And then they tackled the big issue, with Phyllis on the offensive despite her sneaking appreciation. What was there about giving a copy of *Atlas Shrugged* to Andrei—when he had left the tour-bus company but not yet left off driving the taxi—that had transformed him into a billionaire entrepreneur? And what was there about giving him a copy of *Atlas Shrugged* that had made Ilse actually expect Andrei to pick up the tab for her assisted living? What a terrible book! Had he actually managed to get through it? Had he laughed his head off? Had Ilse herself ever read it? If she hadn't, what *was* she thinking, and if she had, why had she given it to him? Why in the world had she given a poor Russian taxi/bus driver a copy of *Atlas Shrugged*?

It's hard to imagine that he read it, isn't it? Rachel admitted. But Ilse may have felt that the novel would help him attain his really amazing success because even though it takes place in New York it's really about life in the Soviet Union, a terrible place, and maybe Andrei, in 1991 or so, would still need to be encouraged to move beyond that world as it's shown at the end of the book, a culture with its motor broken. Rachel continued to defend Ilse's gift and Andrei's accomplishment and hence indebtedness: *Atlas Shrugged* shows what was wrong with the Soviet Union, even if it's called the United States, and it must have helped him decide to be independent and rely on himself and make as much money as he could selling whatever. It's a book that undoubtedly helped him get rid of any traces of socialism that might have survived floating around in his bloodstream. It's a book that encourages free enterprise. It insists it's okay to make money, and maybe if you'd grown up in the Soviet Union you might still not understand, well, no, *feel*, that it is perfectly okay to make billions, or at least better than sitting around mourning the end of Communism. It's a book that says trade is the highest human activity and the trader is the highest form of human being and this means you have to have something to trade, copper, oil, railroads, something.

Well, maybe, Phyllis conceded. And it also insists that it's okay to love anyone you want to, even if they're married to someone else or even if they're just someone who's more charismatic than the last person you slept with and you thought you were going to love forever: You know, don't worry, everybody makes mistakes, do whatever you want. It's a book that conveys every human's right to sexual and emotional freedom—

Yes, it certainly has its points—

—but it's still the worst book I've ever read, Phyllis countered. It's the longest, worst book I've ever read. And I still don't see why Ilse expected him to help her out after he'd read it. Unless she thought he was so stupid or so good-hearted he either wouldn't get the point or wouldn't apply it to her. I mean, *it's a book about not helping anybody*: I SWEAR BY MY LIFE AND MY LOVE OF IT THAT I WILL NEVER LIVE FOR THE SAKE OF ANOTHER MAN, NOR ASK ANOTHER MAN TO LIVE FOR MINE.

My God, you actually memorized that! Well, yes, admitted Rachel, surprised at Phyllis's atypical energy, all that's true. But maybe she thought he'd understand and yet make an exception for her because it's so flattering to have someone who's older and more sophisticated than you are think you could be influenced in your life choices by a book, even a bad book.

Okay, Phyllis challenged, then why didn't she give him a copy of *On the Nature of Things*? It says everything Ayn Rand says, in fact it probably gave her every idea she ever had, and it's only 8,000 lines long. And it would be even more flattering for an older, sophisticated woman to give you a Latin poem. Although, of course, it's probably been translated into Russian.

Well, maybe Ilse didn't know Lucretius? Or maybe she did and realized how hard it is to read, even if it's translated.

Well, it couldn't be any worse than slogging through *Atlas Shrugged*. *Why* did Ilse give Andrei *Atlas Shrugged*? Or, a more important question, insisted Phyllis, who felt she'd suffered a life of masculine underappreciation, infidelity, and insufficiency: *Why didn't he pay?* Why didn't he pay for her assisted living? He wouldn't even have noticed the money. Whether he believed Ayn Rand or not, so what? Who bases what they do on a tenth-rate novel?

I guess that's true, but there was a good reason for his negligence that has nothing whatsoever to do with the book. Rachel was now proceeding with dignity.

Well? said Phyllis. I'm waiting.

This year, after Ilse had been in assisted living for about six months, she got a letter from Andrei's brother, Vladimir, who, I guess, had ended up with a pile of her letters, and he explained that Andrei couldn't answer them because he'd disappeared, simply vanished from the face of the earth. That's why he didn't pay. One day he was sitting in his office in some big building in downtown Moscow. And the next day he was gone. He probably didn't even know she'd been asking for help.

And the notion of Andrei's disappearance was so ridiculous that the friends started laughing. They didn't think about dank prisons and court appearances in wire cages. They didn't think about ransacked offices, confiscated houses, uranium poisoning, limited rations, and untreated medical emergencies. They didn't think of anything like that, and so they couldn't stop laughing. All they could think about was Andrei seduced by John Galt and lured off to Galt's Gulch, living in the pastoral paradise of the hidden valley and leaving the world to fall apart all on its own without the help of the movers of the universe, the Atlases of the world. Had John Galt come in person to spirit Andrei out of Moscow?

They were laughing so hard they didn't even notice the shudder of indifference, the sudden roar of clashing materials, the jolt. They were laughing so hard that when the car skidded off the road they didn't even have time to get scared. It could probably have tumbled over the cliff and they'd have gone laughing to their graves, not a bad way to end things, but they didn't go over the cliff because they were on the village, not the cliff, side of the road. And so they just ended up sitting there laughing, two old ladies laughing at *Atlas Shrugged* and the ironies of new Russian capitalism.

It happens all the time, Phyllis explained, you get used to it after a while.

I could never get used to it, Rachel confessed. I think you ought to move back to D.C. We could have a book club.

This made them laugh even more, but once they calmed down they got back on the road and drove on up to Trinidad to visit Lucinda, who—it turned out—was pretty happy in assisted living, much more optimistic than when they'd seen her last, rid of the helpless help and the sight of those awful trailers in the parking lot. To pass the time while they ate their little cakes and drank their tea, Rachel told Lucinda the story of Andrei and Ilse, and when Phyllis started to give Lucinda the copy of *Atlas Shrugged* she'd brought along for the purpose of trouncing Rachel with quotations, it turned out that Lucinda had read *Atlas Shrugged* years ago, and she'd recently read *The Swerve* and was rereading Lucretius. And when Rachel started criticizing Lucretius's science—after all he had no sense of energy and even if he did influence Galileo and Bruno surely someone would have come up with atomic theory even if he'd never written a line and after all it was Epicurus, or was it Democritus? who'd come up with the original idea— Lucinda pointed out that it's not the specific scientific facts that are important so much as understanding that there's a natural explanation for everything and hence no need to invent a supernatural power to explain everything. Simply observing Nature and her laws is enough to understand the nature of things, Lucinda pronounced, and Rachel and Phyllis certainly agreed with her, and as they drove back down to Mendocino along the dark and swerving road, indifferent for the moment to their own inevitable fates, they each felt they'd missed some fact about Andrei and Ilse. Not a supernatural fact, just a scientific fact, but missed all the same.

After her visitors left Lucinda sat there remembering how the motor of the world stops all the time and then kicks in again and debating whether she'd watch a few more episodes of the 1970s television version of *Tinker, Tailor, Soldier, Spy* on DVD or settle in with David Ignatius's latest. As she debated she tsked her tongue and smiled her most condescending smile and thought about the ease with which

Rachel and Phyllis ignored the obvious, and then she ate another little cake and wondered how they'd have reacted if she'd told them that old and undoubtedly apocryphal joke about the fan who'd asked Le Carré what his favorite food was and he'd answered Red Herring.

The Ghost Driver

Let me tell you a story about how we became the success we are today.

A number of years ago my husband left me to marry his girlfriend. I couldn't blame him, really. Things had been cool between us for years, and from all reports she was as earnest as he was. You could imagine them wincing together over the vulgarities that make up modern life. Many divorced women of my age and circumstances in Washington go into real estate as a way of maintaining their customary standards of living. I found myself totally uninterested in real estate. I moved into an efficiency in the neighborhood and left my husband and his girl an eight-bedroom house, two golden retrievers, a young parrot, and four children in college. All of them, including the parrot and the girl, could visit me if they wanted to, but from now on they had to maintain their own standards of living. I was going slumming. My friends have always laughed at my *nostalgie de la boue*, a taste I can't deny. To me, the most luscious cheeses, the most beautiful flowers, the best wines all savor of decay. Let my life be garbage: I decided to become a ballroom-dance teacher.

Many such establishments flourished in my youth, the Arthur Murray Dance Studios, for example, or those of Fred Astaire. I, of course, had never set foot in one (my dance instruction took place in Lake Forest courtesy of Mrs. Hobson and her sidekick, Mrs. Taft), and for all I knew those chains had long since gone under. So the focus of my desire was a small studio on the second floor of a nearby commercial row. This strip—and its centerpiece, the Park and Purchase—had recently been threatened because a new subway stop had attracted apartment-house developers. Historic preservationists had rushed to the rescue, and the whole neighborhood had rallied around. Indeed, it was during this campaign that my husband found true love at last.

If the P&P lacked architectural distinction to the everyday eye, it possessed historical significance because it was the first supermarket in the galaxy where you could park your car while you went in to shop. Not that it really worked. The only reason people had patronized the P&P in recent years was because it delivered. Nevertheless, we (my husband and I plus a hundred or so others) argued that we should cherish such relics of the recent past, no matter what they looked like. In this, as in many things, my husband and I almost saw eye to eye. To me, the P&P had the nutty appeal of a theme park; I could virtually hear the Park Service guide of the future: "And this is a *manual* cash register!" My husband and his girl, on the other hand, were drawn to the more serious economic argument that all the little shops would go under when they had ten floors of apartments and office buildings perched on their shoulders. Rents would skyrocket. Neighborhood amenities would disappear. In any case my meager part in this battle endeared me to Reggie when I first got to know him, and that, after all, was where my ultimate interest in the shopping strip lay: in the Reginald Majesty Dance Studio, high atop Helen's Dresses, next door to Ben's Barbershop. During the demonstrations I had wondered about the sign a hundred times.

When I thought about it later, I realized that I had expected the studio to be worse than it was. Someone—the receptionist, perhaps—had gone out of her way to fix things up, adding such touches as the half-dead philodendron that insinuated itself among the dusty venetian blinds, the fuzzy toilet-seat cover in the Little Girls' Room, and the telephone message pads decorated with kitten paw prints. Bleached blonde curls, turquoise lids, silver heels, and a red mini, Brenda herself was too good to be true, and Reggie was everything I'd ever hoped for and more, sleaze personified: my age, maybe five years younger, dyed black hair, mud-colored skin, ginger eyes, a thick urban accent of some sort, and a closetful of iridescent suits that looked as if they'd been spun out of beer cans. He even used Old Spice.

"You never took any real dance lessons?" Looking me up and down, he seemed to find my ambition only a little less unbelievable than my appearance: a gaunt, leather-skinned, pale pale blonde in a ratty tweed suit and pearls. "Well, let's dance," he suggested.

He turned out to be the gentlest, smoothest partner I had ever had, leading me through my paces firmly and calmly, always letting me know what he wanted by signs so subtle that I was over the fence before I noticed I'd left the ground. I knew I was no match for him, but after the record stopped (an early Artie Shaw) he said, "Yeah, well, you're the real thing, all right."

Yeah, well, I'd known it all along. The job was mine.

When I got to know Reggie better I decided he looked like the guy in *Seven Samurai* who looks like Buster Keaton. Long and hard, hollow-jawed, hooded-eyed. Steals a gun, kills a few bandits, falls asleep. The young student samurai tells him that he really admires him. Reggie, Samurai of the Dance. He'd always been wild about dancing and had actually gone out to Hollywood to see just how far his skill could take him. Then he'd worked for an Arthur Murray studio in the Midwest, managed a motel in Pennsylvania, and, when his wife's father died, invested her inheritance in this small business in a livable environment. Now, at last, he was going rapidly broke.

His wife had been the receptionist and done a little teaching until two years before, when she'd died of cancer. Brenda, her unofficial replacement, couldn't dance a step, unfortunately, for staff was expensive, and on the face of it she was the sort to fulfill any number of clients' dreams. The rest of us worked part-time: Eduardo, Kiti, and me. Eduardo was tiny, elegant, from a good family in Ecuador, working to save money to go the University of Virginia in the fall. Kiti, whose name probably means "sweet" in Bengali, was enormous with beautiful manners and the graceful moves fat people sometimes have. Her father was a rich tea merchant in Calcutta. Eduardo and Kiti were wildly in love, having met at Reggie's several years before. Kiti's husband, who worked for the World Bank, felt he had nothing in common with her (they were childless) and suggested ballroom dancing as an interesting hobby as well as a useful skill. Eduardo was Kiti's instructor, and the rest was history. Spurred on by passion, Kiti took so many lessons she was soon capable of teaching others; then she left her husband. She was thirty-eight; Eduardo was twenty-one. To make ends meet, Kiti also did telemarketing for the *Washington Times*.

Their story was almost illustrative. Few, if any, of our customers hankered after raw sensual contact; most lusted after spiritual goals: Latin American charm, Eastern mystery, WASP respectability, and so on, all of these qualities mingling into a million different reasons to take dance lessons. However, after I'd worked at Reggie's for about a month, Eduardo went off to college and was not replaced, leaving Reggie to serve all female fantasy with Kiti and me (part-time) for the men.

There might be a million reasons to take ballroom dancing, but that didn't mean we had a million customers. In truth, we had very few indeed. In the past, Reggie had attracted the old ladies from nearby apartment buildings, but whether dead in their graves or satiated with romance at last, most had ceased to take lessons. The World Bank/ Embassy/IMF folk had also dwindled away—whether repelled by Kiti's disaster or subject to a growing conviction that ballroom dancing was of negligible social value. A few couples hung on, not enough by any means, and some days it seemed to me that we were part of a commercial strip that was simply servicing itself—cutting its own hair, eating its own lunches, cleaning its own clothes, repairing its own shoes, and teaching itself to dance. I worked primarily with Sergeant Gibbs of the Metropolitan Police Department, Wu of the Chinese restaurant, Syd the pharmacist, and a middle-aged Iranian from the local branch library. Mine was a very part-time job, and Kiti gently brought up the possibilities of telemarketing.

Still, I couldn't complain. After years of raising children, playing tennis, and walking dogs, I found dancing for a few hours a day not the least bit strenuous. In fact, once my pupils had learned the basics, my job consisted of . . . dancing and a little aloof conversation, since no one expected warmth from someone like me. The only thing that made me nervous was the vision I saw in the sectional mirrors on the studio walls: me—blonde, lean, a prunes-and-prisms expression on my face—circling around the varnished floor, pushed backward by a series of more or less intense, fattish, rumpled men, all several inches shorter than I, all happy to have conquered America at last. Why did this vision disconcert me? I have never entertained a political conviction in my life.

It did occur to me that business was bad, even before Reggie revealed his two scenarios for expansion. One was to turn the whole thing into a massage parlor. The other was to move into children's classes, offering instruction in manners and deportment as well as dance. I argued—with remarkable restraint and absence of irony— that the neighborhood men would not frequent such an establishment close to home, while none of the submerged ninety-nine percent would come over to this side of Rock Creek Park to get massaged. As for the other notion, even Reggie could imagine the problems. I can see him now in his beer-can suit, his patent-leather shoes up on his desk, his after-lunch toothpick traveling to and fro between his lips, rainbows radiating off his hair: "Well, yeah, I know you're thinkin, Who would come here to learn manners? 'Yeah, sweetie. You want your kid should talk like me? Give me five hundred bucks, and I'll throw in the dancin for nuttin.' I know, I know. I'd hafta hire some more upscale dames like you."

"You bet," I said. "We're a type. We probably hang out at a bar somewhere. There's probably a street in Paris chock-full of us."

Of course Reggie was just teasing, and yet I did get a little irritated because while the women who do children are a type, it's hardly my type! Creatures from the margins of respectability, they actually believe in the whole thing! How could Reggie mistake me for one of them? Even in jest! "Mrs. Forbes has that market sewn up in the District," I said with great restraint.

"Then we'd better pray for a new Fred Astaire movie, sweetheart, cause the wolf is at the door."

I suggested he buy a little advertising, but he said it was a waste of money, and out of the blue, we did attract Mr. and Mrs. Grimes, who ran the local junk store. I thought it was curious that they'd fall for the glamour and excitement of ballroom dancing until I caught Reggie "investing" in a Ming-style vase.

Still, for me, dancing was if not meat on the table at least Worcestershire sauce, and I'd never been so happy in my life. Ma Bohéme!

This brings me to that red-letter day on my calendar, December 12, the day we became successful. Things began badly. No sooner did I get to work, around four, than Reggie and I had an enormous fight, triggered by some explosive news. The P&P had been judged lacking in historic as well as architectural worth. The whole strip was doomed to be leveled and replaced by a huge, characterless building full of yuppie hordes, who would clog the streets on their way to and from work and cause enormous parking problems in the interval. Reggie was distraught. But why take it out on me?

"You won," he bitterly announced.

"But I'm on your side," I reminded him.

"Who profits from development except rich people like you?" he shouted as he turned on me, reverting to more-or-less Standard English as he always did in times of stress. "You're the ones who own the investment companies and the banks! And all those big houses you want to protect. You claim you want to save us, but all you really want to do is keep the neighborhood quiet and make sure you have lots of on-street parking. You claim you want to save the P&P, but what you really want to save is the world of your childhood when your mother drove you to the supermarket in a station wagon full of cocker spaniels. To you, it's Nostalgia City. To us, it's life."

"Look! I fought to save this place too. I even lost a husband in the battle. You just can't admit that nobody wants the services you think you're providing. Nobody wants to have his hair cut by a lousy barber. Nobody wants to buy dowdy dresses from a frump in a wig and a gir-dle. Nobody wants to learn ballroom dancing."

"Who wants to be a theme park where some useless twat acts out her fantasy life?" * "If you don't want me slumming in your studio, don't make it such an inviting slum." * "Snotty bitch!" * "Lazy ass-hole! You even pay too much income tax!" * "You rich people live in a dream!" * "Yes! You are the dream, and you are extremely fortunate we're willing to dream you."

Et cetera.

Brenda and Kiti tried without success to calm us down. When we got around to repeating ourselves the third time, Reggie fired me, and I would have walked out had we not found ourselves in the grip of an urban problem more compelling than rampant real-estate develop-ment: Snow was coming down fast. During the course of our quarrel, an inch had accumulated. It was rush hour. The city was paralyzed.

In the street below us, a salt truck was wedged behind a bus that had roared into the intersection on a yellow light. The truck, in turn, had been hit by three subcompacts that couldn't stop. Avoiding rear-end collisions, two vans had braked suddenly and now lay perpendic-ular to the normal flow of traffic. Here and there, patches of orderly traffic sat immovable, motors wisely off, the snow entombing them in the peace of the just. Pedestrians poured out of the subway exits and wandered aimlessly along the unfamiliar sidewalks. The Metro had broken down. Something was frozen.

Reggie and I were forced into a sort of peace. I agreed to go for Chinese while Reggie headed for the liquor store. When we got back Brenda informed us that the new forecast was for a foot and people were being warned to stay off the streets because . . .

Somewhere a tree fell and plunged us into darkness.

But not into gloom. If this had happened ten years earlier, I'd have been a nervous wreck, unable to sit down until all the children were accounted for and then unable to stop fretting about stray cats, baby raccoons, winter's birds, and the rest of hapless nature. Now I enjoyed the calm of the deracinated. In fact we all began to feel quite cheerful. We lit some candles (scented, alas!), and after dinner Reggie brought out a bottle of rye and in a gentlemanly gesture of forgiveness offered me the first swig. The spirit of carnival was upon us.

"Let me tell you a story," said Kiti in the Calcutta version of "Once upon a time." Seeing the stalled bus and the abandoned cars had reminded her of a tale she'd heard at least a hundred times.

*

A man named Sami ran a sweet shop that never prospered. One day he made a vow that if the morning brought him just twenty paying customers, he would do *puja* at a shrine in his family's village five miles out of town. No sooner had he uttered this vow than a bus stopped in front of his shop and twenty-five Peace Corps volunteers ran in to buy a Coca-Cola. The next afternoon, accordingly, Sami left the shop in the hands of his wife, took the bus out to his old village, and did *puja* at the shrine. He chatted for a while with a distant cousin, who was happy to hear that a vow to the old goddess still carried some weight, and by the time Sami was ready to go home, the last bus for town had already left.

Sami had no desire to spend the night in the village, and so he started to walk. Town was only five miles away, after all, and the moon was full. But then, after he'd walked for a while, just when he'd reached a stretch where the jungle pressed up close against the road, the moon went behind a cloud, and the thought of tigers began to prowl across his mind. Suddenly he heard a noise. Something was coming up the road behind him. The bus! The bus! But no! It wasn't the bus. A black patch in the darkness, it was too low—and too quiet—to be a bus. Instead, moving slowly, slowly down the road came a long, long, low black car of a particularly ancient make.

As soon as Sami realized it was a car, he leaped into the middle of the road, frantically waving his arms and planning to yell, "Stop, stop!

Ride to town! Ride to town!" But to his surprise, before he could get the words out of his mouth, the elegant car stopped right in front of him, and before the driver could gather his wits and change his mind, Sami quickly opened the back door and jumped in. Seconds later the car began to move again. Inside, it was pitch black, but Sami realized almost at once that there was nobody else in the backseat and so directed his thanks to the front: ". . . all of these Americans getting off the bus . . . and I am vowing . . . and I am going," and on and on he rattled, giving the full details of what had brought him to this deserted jungle road. So taken was he with his own explanation that at first he failed to notice that not so much as a polite "Hmmmm" was coming from the front seat. But finally his tale came to its conclusion, and he waited for the driver to explain how he had come to be driving down this deserted jungle road and why he had decided to pick up Sami. After all, so dark a night, so deserted a road, suppose Sami was a robber? a demon? a wandering ghost?

Sami waited and waited, but no explanation issued from the front seat. No explanation, no reply, no sound at all. How rude! How insolent! Pick up a poor fellow on his way home and then refuse to talk to him because he is only an ordinary sort of fellow, not a rich and powerful merchant, only a simple and honest man, a poor and pious supplicant returning home late at night after a strenuous pilgrimage to fulfill a religious vow. What could be more insulting? Sami raised himself—with some difficulty—from the deep, soft cushions of the backseat in order to lean forward into the front seat and tell the driver what a stupid, uncivilized baboon he was . . . only to discover that there was no one in the front seat. There was no one driving the car!

For an instant Sami thought that the driver had gotten out to relieve himself—but no! Slowly, slowly the trees rolled by the car, brushing their branches against its windows. The car was moving, but no one was driving! And Sami cast himself down on the floor of the backseat and buried his head in his arms, cowering out of range of the Ghost Driver—the Ghost Driver, who was driving him to Hell! Wedged between the seats, he went through agonies of fear, shivering and weeping and praying to every god he could think of, except the spiteful goddess of his village who had caused all the trouble in the first place by sending the Peace Corps volunteers, and then, rage replacing fear, he saw himself as a man unjustly punished for doing good and fulfilling a religious vow, a man unjustly punished for accepting a well-deserved ride to town. But, eventually, came resignation. As for a drowning man, his life flashed before his eyes, and he was dead . . . or waiting to die, waiting . . . waiting. . . .

Cautiously he raised his head from the floor and, peeping through the side window, saw the trees stretch out their beseeching arms at a slant that suggested the car was going rapidly downhill. At that moment the moon burst out from behind the clouds to reveal the Ghost Driver— an empty space behind the wheel!—and nature's brilliant indifference to Sami's plight. Despair! And then, gradually, the car slowed down. Was it possible? Was this his imagination? The downward-slanting trees leveled off, and all at once the car came to a complete halt. Sami seized his opportunity, his one chance! He flung himself against the door, twisted the handle, pushed with all his might, cast himself out of the car, and somersaulted head over heels into the dust of the road.

Perhaps he passed out for a second, but in another he was up on his knees begging for mercy from the creature who came running over to intently scrutinize him by the light of the moon. Not the Ghost Driver visible at last, not the Ghost Driver ready to extract Sami's soul with a pruning hook, but a frail, sweating, breathless, dust-stained servant, who pulled Sami to his feet, patted him encouragingly on the back, and dragged him over to the car: "Oh, I am so happy! I run out of gas, and I pray to the goddess of my village, and—at last! She sends someone to help push!"

*

Well, we all laughed, of course, and I can say, looking back now from a distance of twenty-odd years, that that was the beginning of it all. Not of any romance between Reggie and me, if that's the success you were expecting. In fact, when I fell in love a few years later, it was with one of my ex's boyhood friends—a nature freak, into birds, and very kind. And Reggie continues, even today, courting, betraying, and sulking over a chorus line of Brenda-like creatures. Instead, what Kiti's story inspired us to was forward motion. For all his failure, Reggie was a model businessman; he simply lacked a star to which he could hitch his wagon. And after Kiti's story he suddenly saw that transportation was a star—and, after my divorce settlement, he found willing capital. We abandoned the dance studio and opened first one—and then a whole slew!—of outrageously profitable driving schools. Out in the Virginia suburbs we captured the teenage market, and in Arlington (under Kiti's eye) the sons and daughters of Southeast Asia, and then in Adams Morgan and Silver Spring (Eduardo abandoned the University of Virginia) those refugees from the slums of Central America who sought true escape in the most literal vehicle of the American dream. And so on and on, into the future . . .

As for the dance studio—when Reggie lost his lease, no major wails of customer despair accompanied his departure. Yet after a few years, when the dread buildings were towering on the site, he discovered that they were filled with faceless yuppie hordes dying for local color and willing to pay hard cash for any sleazy dream they were offered, even the foxtrot and the waltz. So we rented some space, and even though Reggie hired professionals, we all dropped in from time to time to tread the light fantastic, and soon the dance studio was making money hand over fist. We were ecstatic. Thank God for tall buildings! Thank God for yuppie hordes! Thank God for development! Suddenly we were rich, and virtually overnight all of us moved out to Potomac, the fanciest suburb around.

Of course, if you are a truly moral sort, you could insist that sites around subway entrances should be devoted to low-income housing for the poor and carless. And you could—no doubt—mention all the old ladies priced out of their apartments by rising rents. And you could even point out the number of local businesses that went under to be replaced by chains. Indeed, you could say that in praising development we rejoiced at the expense of others. And this is true. But then, we are alive, and just think of the dead! Cut off from the pleasure of living, they are as numerous as the moments that sift downward into time. Their joy, dumb beyond feeling, leaches into the soil and washes away forever. Yes, the dead are dead, the past is the past, and every dance in the universe waltzes on a grave.

The Odor of Mr. Fitzpatrick

Every Sunday Mr. Fitzpatrick went to an early Mass at St. Rita's and then came over to announce his return to Mary, who wondered how the other faithful dealt with Mr. Fitzpatrick's body odor. Did they create a doughnut of space around the hole of Mr. Fitzpatrick? Or did they accept him as a convenient leper in their midst? Mr. Fitzpatrick's smell itself was easily explained. He did not bathe, a not-unusual eccentricity of the old, and Mr. Fitzpatrick claimed to be ninety-seven, except on the day when Mary asked him how he was feeling and he answered, "As well as can be expected for an eighty-three-year-old man." Easily explained or not, his smell lingered long after Mr. Fitzpatrick had gone on his way, as if waiting to greet him on his return. What did the communicants at later Masses make of that enduring odor? Certainly it was from this unmistakable sign that Mary came to realize that Mr. Fitzpatrick essentially lived in her house. His stench was a presence in itself, and it hinted of the grave.

Mr. Fitzpatrick had taken possession of her house only after many years, although Mary remembered him as one of her first visitors when she'd moved in ten years before, right after her divorce. Mr. Fitzpatrick had come up as the movers were carrying in the furniture she'd inherited from her mother and announced that he lived in the apartment house down the street, that he was quite spry (being only eighty-seven or seventy-three at the time), and that he was available to help in her garden. Mary's first impression was of someone tall, thin, white-haired, bony, and wrathful, in this way resembling Joyce and Beckett, his fellow countrymen. Who knows what they smelled like?

Mr. Fitzpatrick presented his gardening credentials as an incidental detail of autobiographical explanation. Starting out as a young undergardener on a large estate in Ireland, he had been brought to England by his appreciative employer's best friend, who owned an even larger estate near Bath. Later, after Mr. Fitzpatrick told Mary that he'd left Ireland in order to escape IRA conscription at the time of the Great War, his gardening abilities became the most believable item on his rambling oral résumé. Not that it mattered much. Mr. Fitzpatrick did not exactly end up working in Mary's garden, although he frequently stood in the shade of a tree and carried on a spirited conversation while she planted, weeded, and picked, revealing in these circumstances that he was unable to recognize the simplest flower. Tulips, he nodded when she asked him if he preferred yellow or red. Oh, yes, tulips. Surely we've met somewhere before. Vegetables too left a certain blankness in Mr. Fitzpatrick's eye and an expression around his lips of dried-up, pared-down scorn. Yet Mr. Fitzpatrick knew how to espalier vines and prune small trees and shrubs, and this very specialization with no dribbling over into other categories substantiated for Mary the vast estate and the innumerable undergardeners of first the rich Irishman and then the rich Englishman, although the conscriptive efforts of the IRA remained the stuff of which poets construct legends.

Having once successfully established Mr. Fitzpatrick in England, Mary enjoyed ten years of anecdotes about what he had done while he was there: played professional soccer, read (what?) at Cambridge, raised Alsatians, seen active service in the war (which one Mary never pinned down), and emigrated to the United States, having lost his wife in the Blitz. She had been a wonderful woman who kept a bar in a cozy London neighborhood and devoted her spare time to good works. It was not just the pulp-fictional quality of this last assertion that forced the willingly gullible Mary to question its authenticity. It was all too obvious that Mr. Fitzpatrick's was a life untouched by any woman, killed in the Blitz, wonderful, and charitable or not. Indeed he confessed, on her asking, that his mother had died when he was very, very young, after which Mary imagined him living in a long series of boardinghouses until he arrived—somehow—in Alexandria, Virginia.

Their relationship remained an outdoor thing for almost eight years. As she planted, weeded, and picked, Mr. Fitzpatrick told her unending tales of his life, all perfectly unconvincing to an unkind mind, which she was determined not to have, tales interspersed with long, vehement explanations of various mistaken policies of the Roman Catholic Church. The unwise insistence on clerical celibacy helped bring in many a crop of green beans, and once he interrupted Mary while she was hanging out the wash to show her the conclusive photograph of Pope John Paul II as a young SS officer in wartime Poland. Occasionally these two lines of thought—the autobiographical and the papistical—converged into somewhat unwieldy stories of Mr. Fitzpatrick's years with the wartime arm of the OSS that had operated out of the Vatican. In World War II, Mary was pretty sure.

Having been introduced to an Episcopalian sort of God in her childhood, Mary listened to this religious gossip with constrained indifference. It was really none of her concern. She still remembered the moment on a weekend visit to her then future, now former husband when she accepted her alienation from any sort of faith: Easter morning 1968, and the Reverend William Sloan Coffin sternly and earnestly reminded his Yale audience that in order to be a true Christian you had to believe, literally believe, in the resurrected body of Jesus Christ. He seemed to be reminding them of a challenging duty, a difficult but necessary requirement, and since Mary was pretty sure she'd never heard anything about a historical Jesus, it seemed remarkably easy to believe in the symbolic resurrection of his symbolic body, a necessary part of the myth, really, and not difficult at all, Reverend Coffin. Unless of course he was asking her to believe literally in the literal resurrection of a literal body, and, well, then that was really not something she could go along with. And Mary had thought, Well, that's that. If she were a believer, then she might take an interest, or even alarm, in Mr. Fitzpatrick's concerns, but as it was she could barely follow the narrative.

Eight years of Mary's encounters with Mr. Fitzpatrick took place outdoors. But after all those years of misery, she went into therapy and began to take medication, having accepted the medical pronouncement that her mood was a physical disease. Almost overnight, although not precisely happy, she acquired a dog (emotional tie) and a job at the National Trust for Historic Preservation (relationship to outside world). And almost by chance Mr. Fitzpatrick acquired a daytime home when he generously offered to take the dog out during the day. He knew dogs well, he explained, and even though he had only worked with "thoroughbreds," Aurora showed promise belying her mixed origins. If Aurora hadn't liked Mr. Fitzpatrick, that would have nipped the plan in the bud. But she liked him just enough and no more, reserving her love for Mary while nevertheless clearly, even to the most jaundiced eye (Mary's own), looking forward to Mr. Fitzpatrick's visits, which kept her from accidents and misbehavior due to boredom. Mary felt compelled to give Mr. Fitzpatrick unstinting thanks. After that, for a while, everything was perfect—except for the smell.

When the weather turned warm, Mary left the air conditioner on while she was away at work so that Aurora would be comfortable, and soon her first act on returning was to open all the windows and hope for a strong breeze. Eventually, she bought a fan to create cross-ventilation and even tried various spicy potpourris and flowery sprays. Still, she would awake in the middle of the night, smothered by the effluvium of decay, aware that Mr. Fitzpatrick had spent every minute of the day in her house except for those brief instants when he had taken Aurora out to pee.

Then one evening she began to smell him almost as soon as she got off the subway and started walking home, and sure enough, there he was, pacing to and fro in front of her house on the sweltering margin between the sidewalk and the street. "I have been waiting for over an hour," he announced, "on the off chance that you might arrive home on time."

"Is something wrong? Has something happened to Aurora?"

"Not exactly. But I wanted you to know before you took her out for her evening walk that she had a large bowel movement at noon."

With the most controlled of emotions, Mary thanked Mr. Fitzpatrick for waiting to tell her this. But when she entered her house, filled as usual with the stench of Mr. Fitzpatrick, and found the same message attached to the icebox door—"a large Bowl Movement"—she began to wonder if her medication was deadening her ability to feel guilt, for on the next night, when Mr. Fitzpatrick paced the hot verge of the street, waiting to tell her of the occasions in Aurora's digestive life in tones that implied Mary's fault, she found that she felt only increasing irritation. I do not control her bowels, I do not mistreat or overfeed her, and I am not responsible for making you wait outside for an hour or so to tell me things I would eventually figure out for myself. She only thought this, of course; she could never have said it to Mr. Fitzpatrick's face. She was supposed to be sleeping better, yet she found herself lying awake all that night, fighting the perception that Mr. Fitzpatrick was imposing an obligation on her, the moral equivalent of his festering smell, and the next morning she found herself telling him that although she loved to hear about Aurora's day, would he please wait for her inside, in the artificially cool air, because the subway was so frequently, so unjustly late?

It was only the smell she disliked, she told herself. It was not that she was unsympathetic to Mr. Fitzpatrick's plight. She realized that he had nothing to do all day and very little to live on, and she made the arrangements necessary for absolving him of all responsibility for her disappearing stores of tea, sugar, and soup by inviting him both to use her refrigerator at any time (so overstocked with food for just one person!) and to be sure to help himself to lunch while he was keeping Aurora company. She made a point of showing him where she kept the restocked tea, sugar, and soup, and soon Mr. Fitzpatrick provided himself with a small carton of milk, from which he took minuscule sips (she assumed, given its long duration) along with a measure of self-respect.

As she continued with her medication, dog, and job, Mary discovered that in true neurotic fashion she had mistakenly seen Mr. Fitzpatrick as a problem that confronted her alone. It was only when he helped himself to a pair of shoes belonging to her neighbor that she saw he might be less a personal burden than a communitywide charge. Mr. Burt used the shoes for gardening and, having left them muddy and wet on his back stoop, was amazed to find them gone. "Now, who would take a pair of beat-up shoes?" he complained to Mary, but when he realized who would, he came back and asked her not to say anything: "I guess they were so beat-up he thought I was throwing them out." Mr. Fitzpatrick, she saw at that moment, was not her problem alone, nor was she the Mistress Bountiful who had to rescue him in seizures of noblesse oblige. No, Mr. Burt did his part, and maybe other neighbors were involved as well. But after Mr. Fitzpatrick dog-sat the next day, his lingering smell somehow obliterated any sense of a shared responsibility, it was such an isolating smell.

Every evening Mary would return home to find the breakfast dishes, which she had left stacked haphazardly in the sink, arranged neatly in the drainer but flecked with egg and speckled with crumbs. This puzzled her for some time. Why did Mr. Fitzpatrick bother to do the dishes at all when he did them so badly? She practiced in front of the mirror: "Please don't bother. It's just asking *too* much," but finally decided on the only foolproof solution. She began to get up earlier in the morning so that she could wash the dishes herself. After only a week Mr. Fitzpatrick expressed his thanks. He liked, as he said, "to rinse out" his shirt while he was taking care of Aurora. "I just clear out your dishes and swirl it around in the sink. And then I hang it out on the line for a while and put it on a little damp, and by the time you finally get home, it's almost dry." While wondering why her sink, her water, and her backyard air were superior to Mr. Fitzpatrick's own, Mary nevertheless bought some Woolite, which she placed in a conspicuous position beside the sink. To her dismay, its untouched state proved that Mr. Fitzpatrick set no store by such refinements. Still, she could readily understand that age might deter Mr. Fitzpatrick from frequent trips to the Laundromat, and given his limited wardrobe and unfathomable prejudice against Woolite, it was no wonder at all that his clothes, his body, and her house stank.

For formal wear Mr. Fitzpatrick had a good suit, a tight plaid polyester number that he wore to Mass along with a plaid shirt and a striped tie. These items Mary thought he might actually send to the dry cleaner from time to time just because they were "good." Hence the obvious solution was to increase the number of Mr. Fitzpatrick's everyday garments. To do this she bought four short-sleeved cotton shirts at Zayre's and took them on a camouflaging tour through her own closet. For the National Trust she had to wear dresses instead of her usual jeans and flannel shirts, which were perfectly good and well known to Mr. Fitzpatrick. When she told him she was giving the old flannel shirts to Goodwill unless he wanted them for "puttering around the house" and "working in the garden," he accepted them without protest along with the four cotton shirts, the origins of which he accepted as mysterious. Mary was quite pleased with her ploy—until she noticed that no matter how hot and humid the weather Mr. Fitzpatrick always wore the same long-sleeved flannel shirt, a classic in red and black, once one of her favorites. And soon the smell was worse than ever. Her house reeked.

Then she thought of an obvious solution: She offered to do his laundry for him.

To this Mr. Fitzpatrick readily agreed and from time to time gave her a few garments "to toss in the wash." Unfortunately, the smell remained. It was not in his clothes alone but in him, and sometime in the fall Mary realized that he never gave her any sheets and towels to wash. Never. Maybe he only had one set of sheets, one towel? And what were they like? She was reluctant to mention their absence because she only had a washing machine. She liked to line-dry her own clothes, especially her sheets and towels, so that in the winter she sometimes ended up draping wet items all around the house. Mr. Fitzpatrick's occasional shirts hardly posed a quantitative increase, but what would she do in bad weather with his sheets and towels? It was while she was pondering this dilemma, wondering if the only solution was to buy him some sheets and towels and herself a dryer to dry them in, that Mr. Fitzpatrick died.

One day she came home from work to find a large puddle and a contrite Aurora, and just as she was about to check on the absent Mr. Fitzpatrick, up the walk strolled a priest. He introduced himself as Father Ryan from St. Rita's, and he brought bad news. A sudden heart attack.

"How did you find me?" she asked Father Ryan, who seemed to speak a dialect learned from radio programs in the 1950s.

"Oh, Mr. Fitzpatrick talked so much about Aurora I knew she must belong to a good soul, and I asked him for your address. Now, could you give me a wee bit of help with the obituary?"

This she did and went to the sparsely attended funeral Mass. Father Ryan, with the help of Mr. Burt, had taken care of the arrangements, but Mary recognized that Mr. Burt and her other neighbors as well as the ancient mourners from the parish had all heard so much about Aurora that they looked on Mary as Mr. Fitzpatrick's only surviving relative. To keep herself sane under their pitying eyes, she found herself thinking about her contributions to the obituary: Mr. Fitpatrick's birth in Ireland, his escape from the IRA, his stint at Cambridge, his career in soccer, his interest in gardening and dogs, his charitable bar-keeping wife who had died in the Blitz, his service at the Vatican during World War II. Father Ryan and Mr. Burt had seemed to verify all these facts by having also heard them, although no one could come up with the name of or any facts about the wife, and so her existence had to be deleted. Mary and Father Ryan and Mr. Burt agreed on ninety-nine as the perfect age for Mr. Fitzpatrick.

What was so odd was that in the end Mary missed Mr. Fitzpatrick. It was not that they had seen so much of each other, perhaps an hour or two on weekends, a few minutes at the end of every workday. But they had known each other for over a decade, for almost a fifth of her entire life, and, lying awake in bed at three in the morning, she realized that what she missed as much as anything was his smell, for at first she'd thought she would never forget it, and then, only a few weeks after his death, it was completely gone. She could neither smell it nor remember it, and she realized that her privacy was assured. The grave had revealed itself as the ultimate truth and Mr. Fitzpatrick's smell a simple human intrusion on the universe, a problem not to be solved by faith or good works and convincing evidence that it would take far more than a terrible smell to turn her into a good person. Yes, it would take a much worse odor than Mr. Fitzpatrick's, and, throwing her arm around the slumbering Aurora, she fell back to sleep, regretfully but peacefully abandoning salvation for all time.

Visiting

Jesus commands us to visit the sick and pray for them when they die. Judith seems to remember hearing this from someone, a voice from the past, maybe even someone from her Indiana youth. Raised by atheists and never going to church, she would have had to be told. Or maybe she picked it up as she wobbled toward a ladylike C in the required Sacred Studies course at her Seven Sisters college, although she is unable to recall a specific text. Still, whoever or whatever the source, she clearly remembers that Jesus, in all his various versions, does not just make a suggestion. He firmly commands, and that command is what has floated up into her brain today. It's been two weeks, and so, instead of going over to Brookings for lunch with everybody else on the magazine staff, she gets her car out of the lot and drives to Georgetown to visit Alicia.

She finds an unexpected parking space on N Street and walks across the campus to the university hospital. Going up in the elevator, she surreptitiously examines her fellow passenger, a handsome black kid, somber, closed in on himself. He too is going up to visit someone, and for no good reason she remembers an elevator ride with Alicia forty years ago, shooting up through a fancy building somewhere in New York City to a party given by a friend of Alicia's who'd dropped out freshman year to be a full-time debutante but was nevertheless doing well, with a rich husband and a great apartment. There they were, rising up to some rich girl's party, and suddenly the elevator door opened and there was Huntington Hartford, who immediately commented on how beautiful Alicia was. One minute they were alone in the elevator and the next, there was Huntington Hartford proclaiming Alicia's beauty. And she was beautiful, although of course she never thought of

123

herself in those terms, tall, thin, flat-chested, acne-scarred, but beautiful nevertheless, and Huntington Hartford had seen it the very moment he entered the elevator. He got out a floor or two later, a short, baffling trip, and as soon as the door closed Judith whispered to Alicia, "That was Huntington Hartford!" because she knew Alicia wouldn't know. "And he was trying to pick you up!" No response, so she proposed a slightly different explanation: "He's a famous art collector. He has an eye for beauty. He knows what he's talking about." She knew Alicia pretty well by then, and Alicia's reply was quite predictably something like "Ugh." And that's Alicia, thinks Judith and gets off on the third floor of the hospital, a floor not marked for anything in particular, not surgery, not cancer, an unlabeled place where they put you while they wait for you to die.

Alicia seems to be asleep, so Judith sits down, and as she waits she remembers how they met at their first job after college, a women's magazine in New York City. It was Alicia who taught Judith how to deal with an artichoke, a vegetable unknown to Indiana, or at least to Judith, and, when she went home with Alicia for Thanksgiving, how to handle a soft-boiled egg in an egg cup. She remembers how formidable Alicia's mother was, the daughter of a bishop, the inhabitant of a world filled with artichokes and egg cups and arcane rules for coping with them, a world Alicia was eager to escape, although at the time just how she would do that was beyond her imagining. Still, it was to be expected that her plans for escape did not include flirting with Huntington Hartford in an elevator, while Judith, eager to belong to a sophisticated Eastern world, the precise details of which were beyond her imagining, would have responded in a second had she been the focus of Huntington Hartford's admiration. Who was Huntington Hartford anyway? Forty years ago she'd known that. Now she seems to remember that he was a grocery-store heir. A rich old WASP. Or something like a WASP and then considered rich on what must have been the limited spoils of groceries. Not like computers or petroleum. Tea, maybe? She's read somewhere recently that there aren't any WASPs anymore. That seems reasonable. Why would anybody want to be a WASP? As Alicia can testify, it isn't any fun, and Judith can back her up on that. In her experience many WASPs marry poor whites like herself or, if they're really lucky, Jews, and then they celebrate Passover and their narrow escape from being as limited as their parents. And even more WASPs become Buddhists, or what they imagine Buddhists to be, and suddenly a vision of her former in-laws' dogs gambols across her brain: Max, a golden retriever too stupid to fetch, and the black Lab, Sambo, last of his name if not his kind. Hard as she tries, she cannot remember what Huntington Hartford looked like.

Eventually Alicia opens her eyes. Judith doesn't ask her how she is. Alicia tells her that Ellie has just stepped out for a nibble, and it flits through Judith's mind that for all the worlds they were eager to escape and attain, they have not done very well. Now in their late fifties, they have achieved the unlooked-for experience of foiled expectations. Alicia is married to the rector of Washington's most conventional Episcopal church, and Judith has not managed to hang on to any vestiges of the rich, sophisticated world she married into. After a pause, less to gather her thoughts than to summon her energy, Judith begins: "I know I haven't been here for a while, over a week. I'm sorry, but something came up, and I better explain right away because when Ellie gets back he will definitely not want to hear about it."

"Oh, don't tell me you've fallen in love again." Alicia even laughs a little, and Judith knows she really means, Tell me everything, every single thing. Do not omit a single, solitary detail. And so Judith tells Alicia about the man she met in her new book club—after swearing her to secrecy, especially with Ellie, because while he is probably not a communicant, his fiancée, Charlotte, probably is. In fact she is just the sort of cave-dwelling rich Washingtonian who probably still attends an Episcopal church.

"Oh, no," Alicia says, "he's not engaged!"

"Well, yes, he is. But he's not actually married, and he was totally up-front about it, not lying about it or trying to deceive me or anything. I guess he started dating her right after he left his wife, and he's given her a ring and everything, but apparently they haven't set the date."

"Oh, Judith! How could you?" Alicia asks, happily anticipating Judith's answer.

"It was easy!" Judith thinks a little and continues, "God! He was so amazing, and I knew he would be. I took one look at him, an ex-Episcopalian sitting there in the middle of all those Quakers, and I knew he'd be the best lover I've ever had."

"The Quakers! Oh, give me a break!"

"Well, he's not a Quaker." Judith smiles. "He's an ex-Episcopalian and a Republican!"

"Oh, my God! A Republican! You're kidding. You've fallen in love with a Republican! And the best you've ever had?" Alicia manages a nonpainful groan. "I can't believe it."

"The absolutely best I've ever had," Judith emphasizes, and then she goes on to tell the story of the amazing lover she met at her new book club. "Oh, he's unbelievable. Everyone in this book club is a bureaucrat, mostly in the State Department, but he works in some quasi-private entity that runs housing for poor people, I think. The rest of them are Democrats and Quakers, or at least their children all went to Sidwell Friends—I don't know about going to Meeting or whatever—but he's an ex-Episcopalian. I was careful to ask. And a Republican. I pretended I hadn't driven, and he offered me a ride home. I had to go pick up my car the next day at lunch, but it was worth it. He drove me home and walked me up to the front door, and you can imagine the rest."

But just in case Alicia can't, Judith starts at the beginning, a long introductory explanation about how she was interviewing this guy—the magazine is doing a series of articles on all the board members, you know, articles on the preservation activities that got them onto the board—and this one board member, Brian Simmons, is actually from Indiana, where his parents were Quakers and he's been very influential in saving all the physical evidence of the Underground Railroad.

"Was there any?"

"Well, not a lot. But anyway, he got involved in other Indiana preservation things, and then, when he moved to D.C., he went on the board in part because his job—I'm pretty sure he's at State—doesn't have much to do with history. Which is his great love, he said. And I said, Oh, mine too—more to have something to say than because it's literally true—and I told him how I wished I could make myself read more of it, real academic history, not Steven Ambrose and Doris Kearns Goodwin but real history, and he said that was exactly what his book club did." Because Alicia would know that logically someone like Brian would belong to a book club. Everyone in Washington takes part in a prayer group or a book club, one or the other. In fact, for many years, Alicia's husband, Ellsworth, has run a Republican prayer breakfast for high-level sinners in the Nixon administration, incredibly ancient men who have long left sin behind. "And then he said if I was interested in reading real history, he was hosting his book club this month, and wouldn't I like to come? They were reading Caro's book about Robert Moses, and I said sure, why not? And I ran out and bought it and read some of it at work the next day instead of typing up the interview."

Judith tells Alicia how the next evening she drove over to Cleveland Park, and after describing the boring house and the oh-so-typical living room—not in very much detail, just enough to set the scene— she tells Alicia how she noticed him right away. He was sitting next to her, and believe it or not, he was aroused. It was really weird. He was sitting there saying intelligent things about Robert Moses—he was the only one who really admired him—and he was clearly physically excited by her, excited by simple contiguity or maybe by the feeling that some things are meant to be. And so all the Democratic Quakers dissed Moses, and she was careful to make one sensitive, salient remark, not at all critical of Moses, and then she shut up and didn't say another word. And as soon as the discussion ended he leaned over and introduced himself. "Rod Something, I'm not quite sure what."

"You don't know his name!" Alicia actually laughs. She can't believe it—although of course, knowing Judith for all these years, she in some way expected it.

"Well, yes, I admit it, I went to bed with him and I don't know his last name. But the problem is if you miss it the first time, it's hard to ask because that shows you weren't paying attention. Anyway, I know he grew up in Lake Forest, and he went to St. Paul's and Princeton and Harvard Law, and he runs this . . . I'm not sure exactly what it is, something like Fannie Mae, and they make the smallest of profits by charging all these poor tenants for their cable service. But look, he's an amazing lover and totally respectable, and I'll get his last name the next time I see him. Or I could ask Brian Simmons. I mean, I could call him, couldn't I? And I could say I think I recognized Rod from . . . I don't know, some meeting of precinct captains, Republican precinct captains in the District, but I didn't catch his last name. And I'd be thinking, I hope you didn't notice my car sitting out in front of your house all night or me, the next day, coming to pick it up."

"Oh, no, someone like Rod would never be a precinct captain. It's better just to call Brian and ask straight out."

"You're right. It's not the sort of thing Rod would do. You know his sort far better than I do. But never mind, I'll think of something."

"Maybe Ellie knows him?"

"Oh, no. No, no, no. Anyway, Rod told me about whatever it is he does while he was driving me across the park to Mount Pleasant. And he walked me up to my door," and then she tells Alicia how Rod embraced her as soon as they entered her foyer, a long, long kiss—a lot of very active tongue and a firm grip on her upper arms—and after a while he complained that she wasn't paying attention. "Something like, 'I get the feeling your mind is elsewhere,'" so she stuck her hand down and—

"What were you wearing?" Alicia asks.

Judith has to think for a moment. "I decided to wear a skirt, denim but still a skirt, and my pink-and-lavender quilted jacket, the one I got from that Indian import shop on Wisconsin Avenue? I wanted to look serious but unconventional." Alicia nods. Judith sees that Alicia remembers the jacket, if not the occasion on which Judith bought it. "Remember? We had lunch at that new place and then went shopping?" A long, long time ago. "Anyway, the skirt was a great idea because he just shoved me up against the wall and pulled up my skirt—"

"Weren't you wearing tights? Did he take them off? How unromantic!"

"No, not tights. No. No. Knee socks. Boots and knee socks. Anyway, after a while we went upstairs. At our age you can do a lot more if you're lying down," Judith admits and changes direction. "You know, the most interesting thing about him, aside from the fact that he's sexually amazing, is he's engaged to a woman who bores him to death. He came right out and said he's afraid he'll marry her and then die of boredom. Now, that is something I just can't imagine doing."

"Well, clearly she's got some money."

"I guess that's it. Of course you're right. The head of whatever probably doesn't make a lot of money, and it probably really cost him to get divorced. But still." And Judith goes on to tell Alicia in a great deal of detail what she and Rod did once they went up to her bedroom and took off all their clothes and how Fetters was absolutely terrified and hid under the bed but couldn't bring himself to leave the room. This description takes about twenty minutes, from oral sex through lots of positions to multiple orgasms, and lots of exclamations from Alicia to the effect that Judith will never change. Then Judith says she has to get back to the office.

But in exchange Alicia wants to tell Judith about her last visit to her mother in the nursing home a few months ago, when she was still able to get around. "I brought her some flowers and told her about how I was redecorating the living room, not true exactly but easier to talk about than radiation. New white slipcovers, nothing showy or expensive. And suddenly I noticed how happy she was. She's usually really grumpy, as if she just has to remind me how much she doesn't like being there and how she really doesn't see any good reason for it and how it's my fault, my fault and Ellie's. But that day she kept smiling and looking past me at the door, and I wondered if they were serving something really good for lunch or if there was some activity she was looking forward to. You know, they have little sessions where the aides tell Bible stories and sing hymns and all, sort of connecting them to their childhoods. And so finally I said, 'Well, you're in a pretty good mood today. Is something special going on?' And she said, 'Oh, yes, today's the day Alicia comes to visit! She's such a sweet girl, and I do so look forward to seeing her.'"

Alicia laughs, and Judith laughs. "That's a great story. I hope it didn't make you too sad," Judith says. "It's what happens when they get old."

"Oh, no. It was great just to see her so happy. It was always hard to go see her. I guess you feel guilty when you put them in a home, no matter how nice it is. But, you know, Jesus says we must visit the sick and pray for them when they die, and I'm sure we get extra points for making them happy."

After the visit Judith walks back across campus to pick up her car on N Street. Some of us will marry our proper fiancés and die of boredom, she thinks, and some of us will die from breast cancer, and some of us will go on for a long time dying a little of one thing and another before we manage to die altogether from something specific, and over and over again we will all be conscientiously visited by inept fools spouting vacuous nonsense. She is exhausted and thoroughly sick of herself. The knee socks were a serious mistake. Knee socks! Who wears knee socks? And Robert Moses just didn't reverberate. Maybe next week the book club will read *The Unredeemed Captive* by John Demos because she read a review of that a few years back and it still sticks in her mind. A white girl is captured by Indians and likes it so much she refuses to go back to the comforts of Williamstown, Massachusetts. Yes, she just fell in love with Indian Dick, and then she will tell Alicia how she tied Rod to the posts of her childhood bed and—to celebrate the text—beat him with one of those bright-colored

Guatemalan belts Alicia used to buy for Christmas presents at that shop in Adams Morgan: Remember all the good times we had? Guatemalan belts, fashion statement of the eighties?

She is heading toward the library when she is startled by a huge dark cross shooting over the grass in front of her. It stops her in her tracks. It's like nothing she's ever seen before, the shadow of a cross. She waits for it to happen again, and when it does, she realizes it's only a jet, the shadow of a jet. Not a cross at all. The planes are heading up the Potomac River to land at Reagan National Airport, and as they fly along the river they cast their shadows over the Georgetown University campus, shadows that take the form of crosses. It's a remarkable coincidence, she thinks, something they could use to recruit students. But even though she knows what it is, she waits and watches another dark cross appear in her path and then another and another, and she thinks she may stand there all afternoon, watching as each dark airplane shadow shoots across the bright landscape like the blessing of an unknown god, the unknown god who commands us to visit the sick and pray for them when they die, the unknown god who watches us make our visit and do our tricks, the unknown god who watches over us and listens to our stories, the unknown god who forgives us when we lie.

Irene

Irene was nothing if not sensitive to her location, sensitive, too, to the names of the towns and cities through which she had conducted her personal hegira, and so it seemed significant that when Buck escaped from an upstairs window, the tree where he landed was located in Fort Bragg, some ten miles north of Mendocino, California. Buck made his escape while Mrs. Sanchez was shaking out the bathroom rug, and although she hadn't noticed him perched on the towel rack, she immediately screamed for help and Irene got to the bathroom in time to see him flutter onto the low-lying branch of a neighbor's tree. She immediately ran next door to coax him down: "I can't explain, Mrs. Chin, but Buck's in your tree." And Mrs. Chin, accustomed to mysteries more opaque than this, welcomed her in and calmly watched her run through the house and out the back door to direct a plea at the bishop pine that filled most of the backyard: "What *do* you think you're doing? *Come down here right now!*"

After a few minutes Irene calmed down and began to speak soothingly: "Buck, Buck, listen to me, please, please," and Buck cocked his head and looked down, but refused to fly to her offered wrist. It wasn't surprising. They'd never really practiced the come-on-command trick—or any other trick, for that matter. She'd let him out of the cage when she got home from work, and he'd wander about and eventually land on her bed and start pecking at her earrings, just to drive her crazy, and eventually she'd gently seize him and put him back in his cage.

Irene was surprised that Buck could still manage to fly out a window, although of course he'd done it before, or something like it, at least fifteen years ago now, when he'd flown into her ex-husband's classroom right in the middle of a lecture on Frederick Law Olmsted, and even though they'd advertised, they'd not discovered whose window he'd flown out of. Who'd have thought he still had it in him? Maybe it was the continuing influence of his name, for they had named him Buckminster Freedbird, presumably after one of her favorite toddlers from the year she worked at the day care center shortly after they got married. Buckminster Freedberg, Jr., son of the famous art historian by a third or fourth or maybe even a fifth wife.

A slight gray-and-white speck against the dark green needles, Buck perched just out of reach, looking down at Irene, then fluttering almost to the top of the tree as Mrs. Chin struggled out the back door with a ladder. She was in her eighties and had dealt with all sorts of bad situations. A bird in a tree seemed a problem with an easy solution. "No, no," Irene cautioned her quietly. "Don't make any noise or he'll fly away," and Mrs. Chin clanked and clattered back inside.

Buck stayed put on his high branch, and yet Irene knew he was paying attention, looking down, although probably not directly at her, just at the location of her voice, and she wondered how keen-sighted an old cockatiel could be, old, she assumed, for she didn't know how long they lived or, in this particular instance, Buck's age—although it seemed as if he'd been her bird for a long, long time. Maybe he was all but blind, and so she muttered loud words of encouragement. "Nice bird, good bird, you've got a great view up there. You can probably see all the way to the Pacific Ocean, but come on down, now, come down, and let's go inside to your nice, warm . . . home." And after only a few minutes of this palaver, Buck did flutter awkwardly down, more like falling than flying, but nevertheless landing safely on the next-to-lowest branch. Maybe he'd reassessed his options after a careful look at Fort Bragg: blocks and blocks of rundown houses, an abandoned lumberyard, and the dark gray ocean stretching out to meet the light gray sky.

Irene could tell Buck was definitely listening to her because whenever she raised her voice he sort of bobbed in her direction. It was easy to get and keep his attention, although hard to think of what to say. And so, at first, she decided to tell him about his life, a narrative technique that had always worked with Lucy when she was little and had trouble falling asleep. "Your name is Buck Freed—no, your name is Buck, and you live with me in a room on Mrs. Sanchez's second floor, next door to Mrs. Chin's boardinghouse in foggy Fort Bragg, California. Mrs. Sanchez does not technically run a boardinghouse because she has four real apartments, albeit small ones that share a bathroom, while Mrs. Chin has a boarder or two in every room, mostly Hispanic but other things too. You are perched in her bishop pine, a big dark tree, and if you look over you can see the bathroom window you flew out of, and if you look down you can see me, Irene, who has owned you for at least fifteen years now, ever since you flew in the window of a classroom at American University in Washington, not Washington State but Washington, D.C., the District of Columbia, a whole continent away from Fort Bragg and the spiritual location of patriotism, something you'll never have any use for. And then you lived in the District with me and Frank and Mrs. Robinson and Coocoo and Ka-choo and your friend Lucy. Frank's a thing of the past, as are Mrs. Robinson, Coocoo, and Ka-choo, and quite a while ago we sent Lucy back to her father so she could go to a good private school and get into college and law school, but your friend Sinister is part of our household, and she's back in the apartment right now, no doubt wondering where you are."

This yammer seemed to work. If Buck wasn't necessarily listening closely, he was at least taking in the sound of her voice, and he wasn't going anywhere, so when Mrs. Chin brought out a white plastic chair, Irene sat down and, directing her voice at the next-to-lowest branch, went on to tell Buck what he ate and about his home, "a cage in my bedroom, a big airy cage, so big it's less a cage than a room in itself, a room with several perches and your water and seed trays and newspaper spread on the floor. I used to use pages from the *New York Review of Books*; they were the perfect size and if you were a different creature from what you really are you could have read them and then reviewed the books in your own way. Now I just use whatever Mrs. Sanchez throws out. And then there's Sinister, a pale violet Siamese cat we acquired quite a few years ago now, in Lynchburg, Virginia, and she sleeps on a folded towel on the top of your cage and dangles a paw down through the bars, more to be friendly than anything else, because she always remembers that you peck when she gets too close. And when you're out of your cage, she's absolutely terrified of you."

It was the late afternoon of an autumn day in Northern California, not all that cold, no fog to speak of, and after a couple of hours Mrs. Chin took over and muttered Chinese nonsense words, probably meaning *Nice bird, good bird, why don't you come down and stop all this fuss*, while Irene ran over to her apartment, peed, fed Sinister, put on an extra sweater, and grabbed a book, a flashlight, and a bottle of vodka.

133

And when darkness fell, one of Mrs. Chin's boarders, Bobby, brought Irene a blanket, although it still wasn't particularly cold.

Irene had intended to read to Buck since the sound of her voice would keep his attention no matter what it was saying, but after she'd read descriptions of several murders it struck her as inappropriate to be sitting out in the dark in Mrs. Chin's backyard in Fort Bragg, California, reading about the murders of several hundred women in Ciudad Juárez, murders maybe still going on, albeit with Mexican victims, as far as Irene knows, and so not personally threatening. Besides, it was unbelievably difficult to hold the flashlight and turn the pages and drink from the bottle of vodka, and she didn't think it would make any difference to Buck what he was listening to, so she might as well talk. "I wish I knew some Chinese or Spanish," she apologized, meaning some language musical and nonsensical, to him at any rate, a language that lacked the danger of straying into awkward words like "free" and "cage," "but I've never been good at learning foreign languages. So here I am almost an old woman, stuck with English and no soothing foreign nonsense words. And really an awkward command of English because why did we ever name you Buck Freedbird? How could we have forgotten that in essence you are not really a free bird? Although, really, what's in a name? Oh, Buck, Buck," she crooned, "what's in a name? We live in a world where names lose their meanings all the time, which is depressing in a way, although in another way it sets us free because a name is a terrible cage to get stuck in. And yet," she rhetoricized, "do we really want to be set free? Free to live in a world where names don't mean what they say? What kind of world is that? What kind of world are we living in? And was it any better when names meant what they said? When Frank and I bought our house we went to the bank and the loan officer was named Mr. Sharkey and we laughed so hard he gave us a mortgage. And right after I had Lucy, years ago now but slightly before your time, I got so tired of infanthood that I stuck my fist through the bathroom wall and had to go to the emergency room, and the doctor on call was Dr. Payne, Dr. Peter Payne, and I was the only one who thought that was funny. In fact nobody else seemed to notice, including Dr. Payne. About two years later I read in the *Post* that he'd hanged himself, and somebody told me, I can't remember who, it was because he'd fallen hopelessly in love with a television anchorwoman who didn't reciprocate his passion. Poor Dr. Payne. Maybe he was thinking of his name at the end, and maybe she thinks of it still, although I doubt it. Once the meaning of a name goes, it goes for good. Which, as I said, is sometimes not altogether bad, and it's not just the names of people and animals that get lost. Let me tell you a story about Frank."

But before she could launch into her tale, Mrs. Chin came out to relieve her again, and Irene ran over to her apartment and called Stuart and told him her bird had escaped and she was going to be late tonight. In fact she probably wouldn't make it at all, but she'd come in as soon as possible tomorrow morning and he could count on her to clean up before they opened for lunch. When she returned to the chair in front of the bishop pine she picked up where she'd left off. "Frank—my ex-husband—I'm sure you remember him. Tall? Thin? Disappointed?—he belonged to a senior society at Yale. It sounds ridiculous, I know, but the boys all took it very seriously. You had to amount to something to get 'tapped,' as they called it, or at least you had to amount to something in terms of Yale undergraduates, and then they met every Thursday and Sunday night all year long and told each other their life stories. And there was always somebody in the closet and somebody from the wrong side of the tracks and somebody who really wasn't very smart and they'd all been fooling everybody for years, and now they got a lot of pleasure out of confessing and then discussing their secrets at length, not to mention casually pointing out all their special accomplishments along the way, because it really meant something to sit around the 'tomb,' as they called it, and talk about whatever it was they talked about. At that age everybody thinks his autobiography is significant or will be, and it's wonderful, you know, really self-confirming when an institution is set up to validate that belief, and so the whole experience was very important to them. Later, when the boys got married they'd meet with their 'tombmates' in some room attached to the church and get married a second time in a special ritual performed in front of a skull. Some said it was Geronimo's, although I'm not sure how they knew. But, yes, me too. I got married in front of Geronimo's skull in spite of the fact that just moments before I'd fallen in love, really, really fallen in love, for the first and only time in my life, although that's another story, and the story I want to tell you now is how every spring in Washington somebody gives a cocktail party for all the 'tombmates' who live in the area, the old CIA spies always showing up first and hanging out in one corner of the living room as if nobody will notice them if they only stick together.

The best party I went to was at this senator's house in Georgetown. He was an old, old man in a wheelchair and his wife was dead and he lived alone in this big house and for some reason he'd decided to host that year's party. As a senator he'd had one famous vote, against the Vietnam War, I think it was—although to be fair probably more than one if you paid attention to politics, which I never did—and there we all were, pretty much the same people this year as last, the spies off in a corner by themselves. And Buck, the other Buck, wasn't there, probably because he was avoiding me. Anyway, as the party was coming to an end, Frank and I said our goodbyes, thanking the senator and all, and just when we were almost out the door he shouted, 'Don't forget me! Don't forget me!' And I remember running back and promising him that I would never ever forget him, he could count on me, and I'm just telling you this now because I think all those men had totally forgotten the implications of their little club's name. Because eventually, you know, everybody dies, rots, and turns into a little pile of forgotten bones at the bottom of a grave."

That thought stopped Irene cold, but a nip of vodka revived her, and she went on to tell Buck about the other Buck, how lots of people are named Buck, but Buck was the one he was really named after, not after the toddler Buckminster Freedberg, Jr., a nice-enough creature although probably not destined for great things. "I named you Buck after the Buck I met at my wedding reception and fell in love with before I went in for my second wedding in front of Geronimo's skull, a fairly grim omen, although I don't suppose I worried much about it at the time, other than wondering why they didn't put a candle on top of it because it would look so cool. I'll never forget it. Buckley Jefferson Finis Davis Buchanan IV. Yes, really, the Fourth. He was the grandson of some famous senator who was named for the President of the Confederacy, one of those names it's hard to forget once you hear it because it evokes such a world of defeat and loss and grief, you know, the essence of things. I was wearing white, of course, a long white silk dress with a long white lace veil and a triple strand of cultured pearls I don't remember what happened to. The thing about Buck . . . Well, where to begin? He was so handsome, and he had such a beautiful voice—he was in some singing group in college, I never could keep them straight—and his voice sounded like a promise kept. Yes, his voice sounded as if he'd fallen in love with you at first sight and he wanted you to know he loved you still and he always would.

And his name reverberated in your heart and reminded you that history is always a tragedy, no matter what they teach you in school."

About this time Bobby came out and draped another blanket around her.

And then she went on to tell Buck once more how she'd fallen in love with Buck at first sight at her wedding reception or maybe on first hearing his name and how Buck had turned into an obsession. Yes, an obsession. She can call it that now. They were living in Washington during the last years of America's greatness, although of course they hadn't known that at the time and just assumed it would go on forever, and "Buck and I met a few times at the Hay-Adams, a beautiful hotel on Lafayette Square across from the White House. It was the former site of a sort of duplex that belonged to John Hay, who was Lincoln's secretary, and Henry Adams, a cynical historian who wrote about himself in the third person, and I remember how one time we went out to Rock Creek Cemetery to see his wife's grave, the Adams Memorial. She killed herself, I can't remember why, boredom probably, but after that we didn't do sex. Instead we'd meet for lunch on Fridays. Usually in warm weather we'd have a little picnic on the Mall, at the corner of Constitution and Twenty-First Street, the place where they eventually put the Vietnam Memorial, sort of in between the Lincoln and the Jefferson, which seemed appropriate to me because my family had fought for the North just as Buck's had fought for the South, although I was only deluding myself because, no matter where we had our little picnic, it was merely the site of my defeat."

By the time Irene got this far—falling in love and living in Washington in the last days of America's greatness—darkness had fallen in earnest and she could no longer be sure Buck was paying attention since she couldn't see him, and so, just to make sure she wasn't boring him, she returned to her first theme, his own life story—who he was and where he lived—and when she'd told him all this several times over and she couldn't think of anything else to say, much to her amazement he began to sing to her. At first she thought she was dreaming, but she wasn't, for he sang,

"Goodnight, Irene, goodnight.
Goodnight, Irene.
Goodnight, Irene, goodnight, Irene.
I'll get you in my dreams."

Well, Buck didn't have the accent she'd always thought he'd have. Instead, he had a soft, high-pitched Southern voice, African American but not from the Deep South, and then she remembered. Of course it made perfect sense. It was just that she'd unconsciously thought of him as a white bird, which was ridiculous because he was literally a small gray-and-white bird with the capacity but apparently no inclination to talk, let alone sing, before this very moment! And she understood at last how the window Buck had flown out of all those years ago was in the District, and of course he'd belonged to a black man who'd maybe been born a little farther South. And while Irene was thinking these thoughts and waiting for Buck to sing again, Mrs. Chin came out to give her a break, and since there came nothing from the tree but silence, Irene went back to her apartment and peed, and when she returned she decided to go on telling Buck the story of herself, projecting her voice into an opaque darkness six or seven feet above ground level.

"I couldn't find a job doing anything interesting, and I had Lucy to take care of, and I spent my days meditating on the Holy Name of Buck and reading a lot and wasting time in many self-destructive ways like calling Buck every day and having lunch with him every Friday. So, as I said, in warm weather we'd have lunch at the future site of the Vietnam Memorial, and in cold weather we'd go up Sixteenth Street to this building that was straight out of Herman Melville, filled with dark-skinned voyagers from every country on earth, speaking every language known to mankind but mainly Spanish. You went through this stretch of dark hallways, and there at the end was an Ethiopian restaurant where we'd have lunch and sit for hours and talk and talk and talk. But it was only lunch. We just had lunch. Why did we do this? Probably because Buck was an English major and liked to talk about what he was reading, which was always something a whole lot more complicated and sophisticated than what I was reading, no matter what that was. Anyway, at every lunch, every week, every Friday, he made it absolutely clear he didn't want to go to the Hay-Adams anymore. It wasn't loyalty to Frank. It wasn't loyalty to his wife. He just didn't want to. He wanted me to call him on the phone every day and have lunch with him once a week on Friday and talk about books and how he didn't want to go to the Hay-Adams. And of course he'd also tell me how I should get a job, maybe as a receptionist at an art gallery, he thought I could handle that, and I knew I really should give some thought to what to do next, but in the end my neighborhood was responsible for getting me into a career with a future. I lived in an old streetcar suburb called Mount Pleasant. We learned about it from a girl I'd known in college who lived there for a while, and we bought a house, thanks to Mr. Sharkey, but, apropos of names, it wasn't all that pleasant when you got right down to it, although I guess you could say it had pleasant repercussions in my life because that's where I discovered my true vocation."

Irene quietly sipped her vodka for a while, and then she told Buck about Mount Pleasant and how she'd wheel Lucy up to Mount Pleasant Street, buy a cup of coffee at Heller's Bakery, and then head over to Needle Park, where she'd sit on an addict-free bench and read a book. And then one night at a party in Georgetown she met a rich old man from out in Potomac who collected rare books, and later she had lunch with him and he brought a few books with him as bait, books he thought she'd like to borrow and then she would have to contact him in order to give them back, among them a first edition of Hemingway's *For Whom the Bell Tolls*. So she took the bait without swallowing the hook and a few days later brought the first edition of Hemingway with her when she went up to Heller's and then over to Needle Park and read a chapter while she drank her coffee and Lucy took a nap. Usually when Lucy woke up Irene would wheel her back home, but today Irene went back up to Mount Pleasant Street and bought a gallon of milk, some bread, and bananas, cheaper there than at the Cleveland Park Safeway and of course easier because she didn't have to load Lucy into the car and drive over to Cleveland Park. But when she got back home she couldn't carry everything into the house in one load. There were only ten steps, but still, and so, choosing the milk and Lucy, she carried them into the house and returned to find that someone had stolen the stroller, a worthless piece of equipment but in this case holding a first edition of *For Whom the Bell Tolls*. Her heart sank until she noticed that whoever had stolen the worthless stroller had tossed the conceivably priceless book into the yard, where it rested intact, completely unharmed. And after that she began to pay more attention to what thieves stole and what they left behind. For example, the thief who stole the ratty Patterson porch furniture left behind the Patterson eight-by-twelve antique Serapi, which had been draped on the porch railing to air. And the thief who stole the Appleby television set left the really beautiful Ad Reinhardt a rich aunt had given them as a wedding present. And then there was the thief who carried a ladder to the Whitneys' house and climbed up and opened a second-floor window and stole their cassette player, which hardly seemed worth the trouble, and then left by the same window, propping it open with a mahogany casket containing their silver flatware (from Georg Jensen and so heavier and more valuable than most flatware and maybe too heavy to carry off).

And there was the thief—"You'll notice, Buck, how these thieves are all named Anonymous"—who broke into her next-door neighbor's house and stole her television set but didn't suspect she'd hidden her precious jewelry in secret places. The next day Old Mrs. Mason proudly took Irene around and showed her the caches of jewelry, in the bookcase behind the novels that began with M (for Maupassant), in a ratty suitcase stuck underneath her bed, and in a plastic baggie in the freezer compartment of the icebox. They never even thought to look, Mrs. Mason triumphantly declared. "It was an education, Buck, the kind of education that really counts. And it came at a time when it was clear to me, even to me, that I'd fallen in love with Buck's name and Buck himself would never love me back, a realization that grew in my skull until you could see the truth curling out of my ears like some terrible kind of kudzu."

And while Irene was envisioning these ferocious weeds, Buck sang again, his voice conveying all the suffering she remembered feeling when she'd arrived at her plan of action, driven by a painful purity of intent possible only to the true lover of an unattainable name:

"Sometimes I lives in the country
Sometimes I lives in the town
Sometimes I gets a great notion,
Gonna jump into the river and drown."

"Yes, yes, you're absolutely right. I realized I was defeated, I was defeated, and so I left town because you can't spend your life living in the nation's capital obsessing over the name of somebody who doesn't love you." And she went on to remind Buck that Lucy was almost five when she decided to leave, although to be fair it wasn't entirely her decision because eventually even Frank realized she wasn't in love with him and kept asking for explanations. Oh, there were so many places to go. How could she possibly choose? "Just think of all the places with wonderful names suggesting so much more than they say: Lynchburg and Pittsburgh and Dodge City and Cincinnati and all the falls, Chagrin Falls, and Sioux Falls and Great Falls." But first she waited until

Mrs. Mason was at the dentist, crawled in a back window she knew was always unlocked, culled a few things from the secret hiding places, loaded Buck and Lucy into the car, and drove to her parents' house in Ohio. She'd been going through some old books one day and in a filthy dog-eared copy of Byron found the map her parents had sent her during the Cuban Missile Crisis so when the bombs started dropping she could find her way home. Her father had marked the route in red pen, carefully taking all the back roads so she wouldn't run into any trouble on the way, and she'd just stuck the map in a book and gone off to English class, where Mrs. Whatever told the girls she did not give a whit for Mr. Kennedy and his crisis and commanded them to write a short analysis of "When I Have Fears That I May Cease to Be," which would count heavily in their final grade: Fair creature of an hour. So she decided to head for Ohio. Better late than never.

"I called Buck to tell him I was leaving, but his secretary told me he wasn't available and took my number as if she'd never heard of me before and said he'd get back to me, but of course he didn't. So I put you in my Volvo station wagon and drove off to what was definitely not a New World. And that didn't really work out. My parents were getting old, and they didn't want to have my failure rotting on their doorstep, so I moved down to Lynchburg because I got a job there. A job. I actually got a job. It was slightly better than hanging. You remember Lynchburg. Probably not well because we were only there a year, in a small apartment, you and Lucy and me. Out of the hundreds of résumés I mailed out when it was clear I really couldn't live with my parents, I found a job as a secretary at a community college." And the community college was hopeless. A ridiculous school, and she could see she'd never be asked back for a second year unless she enrolled in a graduate program, and so she put up a sign in a coffee house and soon she had a house to clean, a house belonging to a prosperous lady, Mrs. Something, who felt sorry for her because she was down on her luck. And soon she was also cleaning the house of that lady's even more prosperous mother, Old Mrs. Something, and the houses of several of her best friends, and soon she'd be running the vacuum and dusting here and there and taking a few minutes off to run her hand behind the bookshelves, and there it was, there it always was, the hidden cache of jewelry—ropes of pearls and coral, gold bangle bracelets, endless gold chains—and then she'd check under the bed, and there it was, there it always was, a ratty old leather satchel filled with silver objects the women had gotten as wedding presents, silver objects to aid in the consumption of food Americans had stopped eating in the nineteenth century. These she left. Souvenirs of Culinary Happiness. And in the freezer compartment, at the back, a little plastic zip-lock bag of presumably even more precious but really quite similar jewelry, itty bitty diamonds usually, jewelry just where it always was, and she carefully culled some of this stuff, just a few things that looked like everything else, and took them to her apartment, where she hid them in a suitcase under her bed while she was thinking about what to do next. Young Mrs. Something adored her, so hardworking, a mother down on her luck. In fact she liked her so much that when Delilah had kittens, purebred lavender-point Siamese kittens, she gave her one of them, and Irene named her Sinister because she looked a lot more like a rat than a kitten.

At this point Mrs. Chin came out and uttered nonsense phrases at Buck while Irene ran home, peed, and patted Sinister on the head.

When she got back she explained to Buck how much she liked to clean houses, and even though the old women never missed the jewelry—why check on it when you know it's safe?—she decided it wasn't wise to work too long in one place and eventually got a part-time job with a textbook publisher in Cincinnati, and pretty soon she'd given up on textbooks and was working, first, for a Mrs. Roberts she'd found through an ad she'd pinned to a bulletin board at a coffee shop and, then, for four of Mrs. Roberts's friends and dipping into their little secret hiding places, and after accumulating a pile she put on the jacket of a pink Chanel suit from a thrift shop in Georgetown and her three-strand cultured-pearl necklace with the diamond clasp, the one her parents had given her when Lucy was born to replace the one she'd lost at her wedding reception, which had replaced the one from graduation she'd lost somewhere or other, and she drove to Louisville and circled around until she found a little jewelry store that looked like all the others where they never asked questions, Pazoff Jewelry, she called it, and there she explained to the understanding owner that her mother had been dead now for five years and she really did need to start getting rid of her stuff, she didn't want it herself, she never wore jewelry except for these pearls her husband, Buck, had given her on their first anniversary, and her mother had left all these little bits of jewelry to her because her sister got the cottage at the lakes. And buttressed by her winnings she next moved north to Chagrin Falls, filled with bitter old women who hid jewelry in the usual places. "That was around the time I changed my name from Susan to Irene, which is not only a disguise but an improvement because Susan is the name of a dullard and Irene is the name of a woman who is in love with and always will be in love with a man named Buck who will never love her back." As for theft, she never got caught, but before she could explain this amazing fact and tell him about all the places all over the country where justice had failed to occur Buck again burst into song:

"I loves Irene, God know I do,
Loves her til the sea run dry.
If Irene turn her back on me
Gonna take moraphine and die."

"Is that you, Buck?" she asked. "Is that really you? And which Buck are you? Buck, the love of my life, or Buck Freedbird?"

In answer he sang again, in a voice without self-pity, a song of love without blame, a song of getting and having, he the lover and she the beloved, he the desiring and she the desired, he the thief and she the stolen.

"Goodnight, Irene. Goodnight, Irene.
I'll get you in my dreams."

It was such an illumination that she passed out.

*

In the morning Bobby gently woke her up with a hand on her shoulder. She was curled up on the ground, stiff, sick. In his other hand lay a large, still warm, freshly peeled iridescent pearl of a hard-boiled egg, and this he handed to her after he hauled her up into the chair, and then he pointed to the tree branch from which Buck now flapped down and seated himself first on Irene's knee and then on her wrist so he could peck at the egg. And Bobby grabbed him, gently but firmly, and carried him next door to his cage, and that was the end of Buck's little adventure. And of course Irene was too exhausted by her night under the tree, too light-headed and fragile, too sick at heart, to go clean up the restaurant, and so that was also the end of life in Fort Bragg. But that afternoon she remembered how Buck had sung back to her the meaning of her life, and so she took heart and, thrilled and validated, remembered how there's always another job down the road, and by the next day she was feeling well enough to load Buck and Sinister into the car, wave goodbye to Bobby, who stood sadly and silently at the curb, and drive on down the road to some other town where she could stage the next act of her heroic tragedy.

Or maybe Irene felt so validated by the voice of Buck that she decided to become Susan again and move back to Ohio, to her old hometown, and get into a treatment program, but of course I have no way of knowing. As for Irene's story, I heard it all quite a while ago straight from the lips of Bobby, who was working behind the meat counter at Mendoza's, where I'd see him twice a week. And then one night we ran into each other at Dick's, a bar in Mendocino ("So few Richards, so many Dicks"), and he told me the whole sad tale of his love for Irene, his neighbor in Fort Bragg who'd never noticed him for what he was and never loved him back. And I think the burden of his tale was how Grace is possible for all of us, maybe not Grace as we expect it but Grace as it overhears our plaints and sings down upon us from above, even if we never even recognize it for what it is, just take it for what we need.

The Trail of the Demon

This isn't a very nice story, but I feel I should tell it because at the time of the assault I lived six houses away from Dawn, and she had so much to say I thought I'd never hear the end of it. It's as if, in some sense, I owe it to her to pass the tale along—especially after I heard more about the whole thing just the other day, that is, some fifteen years later, when I was back in Washington, D.C., for a visit, I'm not sure why. I guess just to see what had happened to Mount Pleasant, the neighborhood where I lived for twenty-odd years, a neighborhood in a city now famous for stalemate, a city that celebrates its inability to move forward. Ironic, you see, given the nature of the assault.

When Dawn was forty-five or so, she decided she had to do something about her weight. Pregnancy, childbirth, child rearing, years and years of schoolteaching, middle age, she could blame whatever she liked, but the fact remained. She'd always been a swimmer, hitting the pool a few times a week, but even so, she finally had to admit that swimming had simply turned her into a whale, smoothing her shoulders, broadening her waist, enhancing her ability to dip and swoosh and glide through the water with so much ease it didn't count as exercise. So she joined a gym up on Connecticut Avenue and lifted weights on the weekends, and she also began to jog. Two or three times a week, after work, she'd come home, change clothes, and run slowly, very slowly, down Park Road to Pierce Mill and then along the bike trail wedged between Beach Drive and Rock Creek Park. She always stuck to the path. Long before Chandra Levy's disappearance, Dawn knew to keep out of the woods and in sight of the traffic. At one point, soon after moving to Mount Pleasant, she'd taken walks in the park every afternoon; protected by her husband's wearisome Labrador retriever, she'd happily encouraged her son to identify wildflowers—until she heard rumors about some black kids who regularly prowled around the woods shooting dogs. Ever since then, she kept to the path. Cars whizzed past on her left, and occasionally she met another runner heading toward her, and she noticed that if the runner happened to be a black man, he started looking innocuous as soon as he saw her coming, twenty yards away, just as she was certain she started looking more capable of protecting herself as soon as he jogged into view. Should anyone have asked her how they managed to do this, she knew she couldn't explain. Maybe they just smiled politely at each other and said, "Hi." She wasn't sure. Maybe she just imagined it.

In any case, during her decade of running she stuck to the path, got off at the back entrance to the National Zoo, and then, exhausted, trudged slowly back up to Adams Mill Road and Walbridge Street and finally to Park Road—a circle of calming habit that helped her forget the trials of teaching upper-school English at a Catholic school and caused her to lose weight. I can testify to that. If the weather was good I'd be sitting out on my porch, and there she'd be, slogging by exhausted, and I'd ask her up for a drink. Yes, I can personally testify that by the time Dawn was forty-six she was slim and fit and running her little circle three or four times a week. And for ten years she continued to follow the same circuit, if a little more slowly.

During those years the population of the block changed. Daphne and José and Simon left and so did all the old Czechs (one way or another). New people moved in, for the most part not all that different from the old ones—that is, willing to live in a not-quite-gentrified neighborhood, and ten years later I was still there, sitting out on my porch in good weather, asking Dawn up for a drink at the end of her run. And, good weather or not, she ran.

During all those years Dawn would occasionally vary the pattern. For no good reason, just to break the routine, she'd run the circle backward, heading out on Park Road, down Walbridge and Adams Mill to the zoo and then along the bike path to Pierce Mill and back up Park Road. Of course on those days, nice weather or not, I missed her. The incident I'm telling you about happened when Dawn was fifty-five, and it occurred on one of the days she reversed herself. Indeed, had that not been the case, the assault would never have happened. Nor her reaction to the assault.

It was the best weather Washington had to offer, a summer day in 1998, the world enveloped in green, and yet the humidity was low, and Dawn was actually thinking when she started out that the day was like her life. You didn't expect the best, given reality, and then everything turned out okay. She was divorced, like all her friends, but Marvin was grown up and successfully through college and enjoying a sensible job in New York City. To be sure, she was a little bored with teaching, but no more than usual, pleased with herself after initially lowering her professional sights, proud she'd found something to do with her life that was morally worthwhile. And thanks to alimony, inheritance, and a thrifty nature, she was comfortably off. She and her ex-husband had bought their house for $55,000, and today it was worth at least $300,000. She kept herself busy with two book clubs, took one carefully budgeted trip to Europe every year, and regularly attended the theater, the movies, and the exhibitions in the museums on the Mall. Once her parents were dead, she no longer considered herself a product of the Midwest, and sometime during this process of comparing her life to a summer's day, she set off, backward for no good reason, trotting down Walbridge and Adams Mill, and then, just before she got to the zoo, the light at the corner of Irving and Adams Mill turned red, and, still a good Midwesterner as far as traffic lights were concerned, Dawn stood there patiently waiting for green. That was when the assault took place, just a block or two after she'd started out, when she wasn't even winded.

This is what happened from her point of view: An arm from behind forced itself across her throat and her right hand was grabbed at the wrist, pulled backward, and forced down a pair of pants where it encountered an erect penis. By instinct Dawn first grabbed hold and then quickly let go of the penis, pulling her hand away, twisting away from the arm across her throat, and turning to encounter a black kid who couldn't have been much more than fifteen or sixteen years old, the same age as her students, a young black kid, fairly light-skinned, thin, wearing a hoodie and a pair of shorts, and laughing, a young black man with an erection laughing his head off.

A surge of fury and an accusation flashed though her mind, although, after the fact, she was pretty sure she hadn't actually voiced it: *My great-grandfather fought in the Civil War. He marched to the sea with Sherman. His brother died in Andersonville Prison. What the fuck do you think you're doing?* But no matter what she did or didn't say, the kid looked her in the face and doubled over with laughter—yeah, I can get it up for anything!—and that really made her mad. She looked around and found what she expected, given Mount Pleasant, an empty wine bottle lying there in the gutter with a lot of other trash, and she picked it up, shattered it on the curb, and thrust it defiantly in his direction. Until then he'd just stood there laughing, proud of himself, feeling no urgency at all either to attack her or amble on his way, but as soon as he saw the shards of the broken bottle he turned and ran off to the left, up Irving Street, running, running, running. She watched him run, jolting along, not running fast, not really running, no, not running at all, strutting really, not running, only pretending to run, showing her how much he wasn't afraid of an old white lady with a broken bottle, laughing because from the back she'd looked like someone worth assaulting. And she couldn't help it; madder than ever, she took off after him.

Irving Street, in the late 1990s, was all brick rowhouses, most of them decent-looking but far from chic. In the late afternoon the street was completely deserted by black and white alike, everyone still at work, no audience for this drama—because Dawn quickly realized this was performance art. He was playing with her, the little prick, the little asshole, because, after all, he was fifteen years old, and if he really wanted to disappear, all he had to do was run. Instead, he continued to jolt, sashay, wiggle, prance, and giggle half a block ahead of her. Every few minutes he turned to see how far she'd come, and if she'd shortened the distance between them, he lengthened it, casually, all in fun, because of course he knew she couldn't catch up with him, gray-haired old woman who should be scared to death, trembling, peeing her pants, and instead was chasing him! Chasing him! Stupid old woman. Of course he knew he was safe from her shattered bottle, safe from her wrath. And she couldn't even give the police a convincing description because to her eyes, he knew, he looked like every other black boy she'd ever run into.

*

And she would have stopped, she would have given up entirely except for the terrible thing that happened to her, the terrible thing she kept trying to explain while she drank her martinis on my porch over the following weeks. She couldn't stop chasing him because she was pushed forward by fury, fury fueled by her own racist opinions, racist opinions so deep and dark she didn't even know she had them, racist opinions that shoved her forward in a rolling tsunami of contempt and hatred, memories of the Black Panthers who lived in the house across from her apartment in graduate school and killed the kid who ratted on them, and the black thief who climbed in the window and tried to steal the silver but only got the television set, and the black gang members who shot two other gang members and left their bodies in the car parked at the end of the block where anybody's children could find them and Lonnie's did, and Daphne's black student who robbed the university bookstore at gunpoint and had the nerve to come to class afterward, and the black student who stole Phoebe's briefcase from behind her desk in her office when she was in the ladies' room, and the fat black guy who lurked in the woods across Park Road and masturbated in front of the babysitters, and the young black man with the machete who crashed through the door and bounded up the stairs and tried to get into the bathroom where she was taking a bath but she'd locked the door so he ran to the bedroom and stole a tape recorder containing a tape of *Der Rosenkavalier* and the next evening invaded two other houses on the block, terrifying the old Czechs with his machete but never actually stealing anything, and the black person (because only blacks lived in those buildings) who tossed the infant out the window and into the alley where its remains were discovered when the Montessori School hosted the annual Alley Cleanup, and the young black men who ran along the alley shooting at each other while she was out barbecuing in the backyard with Marvin, and the guy who murdered Mrs. Neumann, the old woman at the end of the block who'd managed to walk away from Czechoslovakia in 1948 but unwisely left her alley gate unlocked one afternoon in 1990 and, according to her upstairs tenant, opened her back door to a black kid. And as Dawn approached Mount Pleasant Street, with the little prick, the little asshole still slowly prancing ahead of her, laughing and strutting and demonstrating his superiority, just far enough ahead so she could never, ever catch up with him, she was catapulted forward by the memory of James Swann, the Shotgun Stalker, who shot thirteen people, black and white, straight and gay, and killed four of them during two awful months in 1993, the first victims shot while they were walking alone at night and the first to die sitting in the barbershop getting his hair cut, and then Bessie

Hutson in the alley right behind Park Road, right behind *her* house, blood and brains on the gate, and once a white woman got killed the police realized something unusual was going on, not just the usual drug violence, and everyone else in the neighborhood realized the killer was crazy, not just logically robbing somebody or protecting his territory or wreaking vengeance on some rival gang but listening to the voice of Malcolm X, who commanded him to kill people on the wrong side of the park because they were the ones responsible for his assassination, and everyone realized he'd do worse next time, whatever that could be, something they weren't expecting, children, maybe, and even the drug dealers along Sixteenth Street decided to stay home at night . . . and . . . and . . . and, out of breath, more from rage than running, she had to stop at Mount Pleasant Street, bending over, trying to catch her breath, panting and drooling and looking up to Sixteenth Street, where she saw the kid standing at the bus stop, no longer smiling, no longer laughing and prancing and strutting but looking worried because how was he to know he'd assaulted a crazy white maniac instead of a willing white victim? looking just like a deflated student staring at the totally unexpected D+ marked in red ink at the top of his lousy term paper, and where was the fucking bus? And before she could catch her breath and run up to Sixteenth Street and stick her bottle in his nasty little face, the bus came and left, and he was on it, heading north toward the Gold Coast.

The bus left with the kid on it, and Dawn wanted to sit down and catch her breath, but she knew if she did she wouldn't have the energy to get up again. So she dumped her now useless bottle in a trash can, cut over to Park Road, and started the long hike home.

The beautiful summer day was gone, the humidity back with a vengeance, the vengeance of the City in the Swamp, where stealing was legal only if you worked for the government, a city blessed with a ninety percent black population who hadn't gotten the word, and her fatigue melted her fury into bitterness and her bitterness into the disappointments of her life, and pretty soon her own miserable failures were carrying her down Park Road under the high green arch of doomed elm trees, because why was she without a husband when he was the one who'd wanted to get married in the first place? And why was Marvin living three hours away in New York City except to avoid her? And why had she gone to graduate school when it was clear no one thought she was smart enough to teach college students? Barely smart enough to teach high school kids like the little prick, the little asshole, the little predator turned victim, and, pushed down Park Road by a lifetime of failure, she remembered, clear as day, the assault of the famous professor.

There she'd been, waiting for her conference in Mr. Rosenberg's office, waiting for him to call her in and take her to task for her inadequate papers on Joyce and Beckett and Yeats, when the famous professor came in and sat down next to her and touched her upper arm with a finger, like a gourmand checking out the ripeness of a peach, and she thought he was the janitor and decided the best thing to do was simply get up and leave. When she told this to Hannah at lunch, Hannah laughed and laughed and said it was just So-and-So, who fucked all his students, so she better not take his class if she didn't want to get fucked, and then a few days later when she left the library to take a break, just innocently strolling toward the Green for a breath of fresh air, she first sensed and then saw the famous professor/janitor/fucker-of-students following twenty feet behind, stalking his prey, tasty little Dawn, and she decided to take him for a walk like a good French poodle and teach him a lesson he'd never forget. It was so long ago she couldn't remember what streets she'd taken, the ordinary streets of New Haven, heading downtown to a department store, maybe the only one in town, entering through a revolving door, circling the counters filled with lipstick and nail polish and face crème, followed by the famous professor enclosed in the stupidity of his lust, then heading for the escalator and, as she rose from one sea of shoppers to another festering pool, casting a backward glance to make sure Captain Ahab was hot on her tail, and he was, dressed in black, the intellectual hue, dazed and confused and stuck at the foot of the escalator, unconsciously blocking the flow until an impatient woman shopper shoved him forward, and, as he headed upward, he spied Dawn ahead of him, floating like a lily in a pond of leeches, her glance carefully directed at the bustle around her, away from his ascension, although, like good bait, she waited near the top of the escalator until he could catch up so she could lead him out of his confusion and dismay into the true meaning of things. And as soon as she was sure he saw her, she wandered in a desultory fashion through stretches of merchandise, trailing fingers along garments she would never think of wearing, across objects she would never dream of owning, dipping her fingertips into the filthy stream, pointing out the mysterious significance he'd only dimly sensed before. Fuck words, fuck meter, fuck poetry, Famous Professor That You Think You Are, *this* is real! Oh, going around in circles, her scholar understood everything once it had been pointed out to him, and she picked up the pace, touching things so quickly he barely had time to extricate the message, carefully drawing one finger across the tops of a row of soap-opera-blaring TV sets, checking for cosmic dust and spreading her order like King Midas, reminding him that, yes, this is the world, the real world, the golden world of shit, and there's nothing whatsoever *you* can do about it, and she could feel him muttering, Oh, whatever you say, Dawn, whatever you say, I love you, Dawn, never leave me, always take me with you, please lead me everywhere, I'll be good, I promise, you're so bright I'll believe whatever you say. And, after one more crank around the labyrinth, she ran down the up escalator and rushed from the building before he could reorient himself, find her, and continue to follow. And every time she'd seen him around campus for the next two years, she'd smiled and waved, and for the next fifty years whenever she came across his name, she laughed and thought, *And so it was you entered the broken world to trace the visionary company of love.*

And yet she had to admit her arrogance had led her nowhere, and I watched her march past my house, ignoring my greeting and looking drained of all possibility. She sat down on her front-porch step and cried for America until after a while she hauled herself up and staggered inside and called the police, all of them black because it was the District of Columbia. The guy who took her call couldn't help it, he started laughing, You chased him? You picked up a bottle and you shattered it and you chased him? he asked. Oh, lady, you've got to be kidding! And she could hear him struggle not to ask, Wasn't it big? Wasn't it hard? Wasn't it the biggest, hardest prick you've ever held?

*

Over the next week or so, as Dawn sat on my porch and drank her martinis, she justified herself in long conversations with little input on my part. She had very little to say about the assault of the famous professor and the problem of who had assaulted whom, but again and again she mentioned all the black literature she'd taught to her students over the years—Malcolm X and Martin Luther King speeches and all those ghastly Toni Morrison novels—and, even if she never came out and said it, her tone was pretty much, See, I taught all this shit, all *your* shit, and this is how you treat me. But as the days passed and the martinis flowed and she calmed down a little, she made what I thought was a pretty good point: Black and white together, we have indulged in an outrageous admiration of Bad Black Boys, an admiration that encourages black boys to be bad. A pretty good point, and, remember, this was a decade before *The Wire*! But then she went on, rather less admirably, to describe how we justify the badness of the boys because it's based in bitterness about slavery, gone now for well over a century, and lynching, which hasn't happened in seventy years, and the absence of voting rights, which were attained thirty years ago, and all those nonexistent job opportunities promised by the unions: Bad Black Boys whose badness is designed to make sure everybody remembers how badly they've been treated. And then, wavering between understanding and renewed fury as she sat on my porch, Dawn finally remembered how the kid with the machete hadn't attacked Marvin, who was standing right beside the stairs, frozen with fear, and how he'd thoughtfully thrown the tape recorder into a bush where she'd discovered it the next day, *Der Rosenkavalier* intact. And she remembered the cop who'd stood at the bathroom door and talked her into coming out—the first black man she'd ever hugged—and she remembered the black bus driver up on Mount Pleasant Street who used to announce that the last person off the bus is supposed to kiss the bus driver, and whenever Dawn was last, she always did, although only on the cheek, and the black cop who'd come by to tell her she really ought to find an after-school babysitter for Marvin, no matter how old he was, because he'd lost his key and was sitting on the front porch when the kid killed Mrs. Neumann, and the other black cop who'd come by to tell her she really ought to get some roommates because it wasn't safe living alone with a child, and Reuel, the Jamaican student from Howard University who'd been recommended by the American Friends Service Committee and lived upstairs for two years. Yes, it was true, she and Marvin and Reuel had eaten dinner together and watched television together almost every night for two years, and he'd been a young black man and not bad at all. And finally she admitted that a few of those black criminals may not even have been black because no one actually saw them; their blackness had merely been inferred from their crime, and finally she decided she would start teaching selections from the new *Norton Anthology* and also, maybe, some of those long escape narratives that lie at the root of African American literature, "Box" Brown and all. And that's essentially where Dawn was when I got a good job offer in San Francisco and left Park Road, Mount Pleasant, and the District of Columbia far behind.

*

I'm not entirely sure why I went back. It was 2013. Nobody I knew was left on the block. Even Dawn was gone, retired from St. Cecelia's and living in Florida. Well, I just wanted to *see*, even if I didn't like what I saw. I stayed in a hotel downtown and took a taxi up to Park Road and walked along the old block where we'd all once lived, even walked up and down the alley: no blood, no brains, not even much in the way of garbage. Every house was gentrified. No green indoor/ outdoor carpet on the front porches, no cardboard boxes of vegetables lined up in the backyards. A white guy jogged by. One front yard even sported a little stone garden gnome, which in the old days would have been pitched through a window in minutes. A white girl jogged by. I checked out a real-estate brochure in front of one house and found it was going for $1.2 million. Undoubtedly worth it because everything was green and leafy, and yet the block looked like an egg carton with a bureaucratic egg lodged in every little brown cardboard townhouse, and when I noticed the historic marker at the corner of Park and Klingle—an official metal sign with historic photographs in grayish shades of green—I all but ran up to Mount Pleasant Street to find out what the hell was going on. A *historic* marker? To a *heritage* trail? A guy at Heller's Bakery directed me to a hardware store where I got the booklet, a little guide that commanded me to "follow this trail to discover the traces left by each succeeding generation and how they add up to an urban place that still feels like a village," and, always a good girl, I obeyed, starting at the beginning over on Sixteenth Street, where the first marker was located, and dutifully pacing on to the next, visiting all seventeen markers along the Mount Pleasant Heritage Trail, which led me through a beautiful little history of the 'hood, a nifty little history that included "fashionable" Sixteenth Street and the Wilson Center and the Latin American Youth Center and Aurelius Battaglia's pre-*Dumbo* animal murals at the almost-book-free but grandly restored Mount Pleasant Library and the Sacred Heart Academy and St. Stephen and the Incarnation, where Father Wendt invited H. Rap Brown to speak, and the path Teddy Roosevelt took when he wanted to go skinny-dipping in Rock Creek and the apartment house where Bo Diddley once lived and the Stoddard Baptist Home for old black Baptists and my own Czech Row, endpoint for all those wonderful departures from an old country ruled by hatred and terror and the location of "affordable housing that appealed to political activists, artists, and unconventional family groups," and a long text on some family who successfully defied restrictive covenants and Rosemont Center—once a home for unwed mothers and whores and now a day care center—and Jimmy Dean and Charlie Waller and Triangle Park (called Needle Park in my day) and Lamont Park, acknowledged to have "attracted illegal activity," and, yes, yes, there *were* riots in 1968 and 1991 (when you could watch television in your living room and see folks setting fire to buildings farther up the street) and the roar of the lions at the zoo, and I ended up back on Mount Pleasant Street in a state of shock, having faithfully read every single word and carefully looked at every single photograph on the Mount Pleasant Heritage Trail.

Mount Pleasant Street hadn't changed all that much. Still largely Hispanic, a hardware store, a paint store, a few tame-looking bars (nothing like the old Fox Lounge!), a couple of grocery stores, and there I was, standing exhausted in front of Marker 17, the end of the line, when an old woman coming out of a bodega stopped at my side and commented, "It leaves out a lot, don't it?" We laughed, and I asked the awkward question, "Where have all the black people gone?"—awkward because the old woman was black, black and wrinkled and wearing a red bandana and big gold earrings that made her look like a fortune-teller.

"To Prince George's County." She laughed and gestured at the marker. "So, you been catchin' up on the history of Mount Pleasant?"

"Well, I don't know. I'm not sure these signs can be trusted. I don't see anything about that awful fire where all those illegal immigrants died and nothing about that crazy woman who climbed into the lions' den and got killed, and there's only one phrase about the Martin Luther King riots and almost nothing about that war, riot, whatever it was between the blacks and Hispanics in the early nineties and not a word about the Shotgun Stalker."

"And not a word about the Demon," she said.

"The what?"

And that's when she told me the story of the Demon, an old-woman ghost with long white hair, dressed in wrinkled black rags, who roams Mount Pleasant after dark every night and threatens young black youths with a shattered wine bottle and chases them and kills them and cooks them over a fire in the woods near Ingleside Terrace and eats them and dumps their bones in Rock Creek Park. Over the years hundreds of young black men have disappeared.

"Now, why haven't we read about this in the *Post*?" I ventured, unwilling to give in to such nonsense without a fight.

And she answered, "'Cause the *Post* don't know. Yes," she said, almost as if she were citing a long-established text, "the Demon, she chase 'em and she catch 'em and she kill 'em and she toast 'em." And she laughed again, in a way that suggested she didn't expect an old white woman like me to believe a tale like hers, but *she* knew what *she* was talking about, that is, just how much of the truth to believe and just how much of the lie to enjoy.

I started to say there must be some other explanation for the disappearance of hundreds of young black men: unjust drug policies, for one thing. A better explanation than an old white-haired woman with a shattered wine bottle. But then I thought, Who am I to spoil the fun? And so I said, "Well, now, *that* would make some Historic Trail. The Trail of the Demon." And she laughed straight out at that and went on her way with her bag of groceries, both of us clucking our tongues and shaking our heads like the old women we were. And I stood there thinking about the Trail of the Demon, a short historic loop trail with only four markers: *They. Us. We. Them.* They hate us and we are afraid of them and we hate them and they are afraid of us. *They. Us. We. Them.* Even though when you get right down to it, we're all pretty much the same thing.

About the Author

Jane Gillette has published short fiction in a variety of journals including *Virginia Quarterly Review*, *Yale Review*, *Michigan Quarterly Review*, the *Hopkins Review* and *Zyzzyva*, and previously in the *Missouri Review*. She has won a Laurence Prize and an O. Henry Prize and is a past winner of the *Missouri Review*'s Peden Prize.